MÉNAGE

MÉNAGE

by ANTHONY MANCINI

DONALD I. FINE, INC.
New York

Library of Congress Cataloging-in-Publication Data

Mancini, Anthony.
Ménage : a novel.

I. Title.
PS3563.A4354M4   1988   813'.54   88-45470
ISBN 1-55611-117-7

Manufactured in the United States of America
10 9 8 7 6 5 4 3 2 1

This One's For Joe.

I've seen everything twice.

—BAUDELAIRE

PART ONE

Reflections of a Narcissist

What there thou seest, fair creature, is thyself.

—JOHN MILTON
Paradise Lost

CHAPTER 1

The sky over midtown Manhattan is chilly blue and the mood vespertine as I slide behind the wheel of the sports car and press the starter button. The motor coughs, then purrs, and soon the machine prowls, weaving through traffic down Park Avenue South. I wear sunglasses, unnecessary in the dusk, and a colossal frown.

The conference over daiquiris with Mitch has done nothing to buoy my spirits nor to dispel the worries that have been haunting me lately. Oh, I realize that to the world at large I must appear a carefree soul, a dashing figure in the vintage Jaguar convertible with the top down, the wind ruffling my wheat-colored hair (daubed with gray at the temples), insouciance stamped on my chiseled profile. On the outside I must present a very enviable picture, to be sure. But inside I'm a bloody mess.

Why do I chronically paint mental portraits of myself? These are, I conclude with sour satisfaction, the reflections of a narcissist.

The automobile, a feline thing glinting silver in the guttering sun, crosses Fourteenth Street and stops at a traffic light. I gaze at my image in the side-view mirror and, drumming my fingers in time to the music playing on the car radio, wonder idly how many times a day on average I look in the mirror and how much more often I do it than other people. I'm well aware that this obsession with my physical appearance exceeds mere professional concerns, although those weigh pretty heavily on the scale of things now that my acting career has taken a nosedive (subject of the chat this afternoon with my agent, Mitch Rosen). No, it spouts from a deeper and darker wellspring, certainly. Some subterranean place. And it's not pure vanity either. I've got a funny feeling, an unshakeable feeling, that it comes from some primal experience I had, or maybe something in the marrow of my genetic *personhood.* I don't know—it's hard for me to describe. I'm an actor and, by definition, that means I'm not a very deep thinker. I'm an interpretive artist and not a very good one, alas.

Am I really an actor? I sometimes wonder. I still carry an Equity Card (and SAG and AFTRA cards) and a list of fair-to-middling credits on my resume. But I haven't landed a halfway decent role in fourteen months nor had a callback in six weeks of auditioning. All the signs are there, huh? I have a queasy feeling that my star, never of the first magnitude even in the best of times, has begun to decline. Fizzle. *C'est la vie.*

Mitch thinks otherwise, judging at least from the pep talk he just gave me. Oiled by the booze, he made light of my predicament, blaming it on the post-summer doldrums, the ignorance and philistinism of *arriviste* casting directors, a couple of recent missed telephone calls, the recent death of a prominent movie director with whom he had a close relationship—all the usual garbage agents feed to clients to lull them into a false sense of security. I know that he wears over his liquid brown eyes the rose-colored glasses of his ilk. Let's face it, the film and television industries, nourished by the brisk sales of video tapes, are booming right now. But I am competing against a bunch of up-and-coming young hunks. My biggest selling point—matinee idol looks —is fading, which would be okay if I had ever either completely captured the public fancy or really mastered the craft of acting. Having accomplished neither, I can't make the transition to character roles and so I'm losing my toehold on this always precarious business. I have a gut feeling that I'm just about washed up.

The light switches to green, my foot presses on the accelerator, and the car glides down Broadway. Night descends, spreading its ink on the streaky sky, and the street lamps cast an amber glow on the bustling city scene. It is warm for October and a pleasant breeze ruffles my haystack hair. I jerk my head toward the unusual clop of horse's hooves. A mounted policeman rides up Twelfth Street and stops at the traffic light, surveying the flow of traffic. The animal stamps the asphalt and, raising his fine head, snorts impatiently at the bridle. The rider, a middle-aged cop with a melodramatic handlebar mustache, pats the stallion's neck. On the sidewalk two children, a girl of about seven and a boy slightly younger, accompanying an old woman in a wheelchair, gaze in wonder at the horse and rider, an unexpected sight on a Greenwich Village street. The policeman tips his cap to them and lets the children stroke the horse's flanks and muzzle. I drive on, stealing a glance at the scene in the rear-view mirror, then catching sight of my handsome bronze face.

Suddenly a taxicab cuts in front of me and my fender collides with the side of his car. What a nuisance! We pull over. The cars behind honk like a parade of geese.

I get out and inspect the damage. Could have been worse: a busted headlight, a deep dent and a few paint scratches. Still, I'm not pleased. Body shops in Manhattan charge outrageous fees to work on a 1956 Jaguar XK-140. I look around me. Wouldn't you know it: neither the mounted cop nor any of his colleagues is anywhere in sight.

"Whatsa matter, buddy? You blind?"

I glare at him: swarthy, fiftyish, lean-hipped, wearing a soiled gray windbreaker and a Mets baseball cap. His cheeks are ruddy with anger.

"You cut me off," I say evenly, controlling the impulse to curse at him. I guess I feel a little guilty. I should have kept my eyes on the road instead of acting like a living eight-by-ten glossy and admiring my mug in the mirror.

The usual crowd of busybodies, kibbitzers and bloodthirsty urban sharks have gathered on the pavement, regarding us with ironic pleasure, many obviously hoping that we might come to blows. But we disappoint them. After exchanging insurance information with the cabbie I get into the car and drive off.

Passing the bars and boutiques of NoHo I curse my luck. Another unexpected expense. The bills have been piling up lately while my income has taken a plunge. I can't exactly ask Nicole to economize either. That would be like asking a butterfly to turn into a caterpillar—contrary to the secret processes of nature. No, there must be another way out of this financial pickle.

But what? No day job could possibly support our extravagant way of life—the loft in SoHo, the Fire Island summer house smack on the ocean, the fashionable clothes and fancy restaurants, the trendy discos and euphoric drugs. In a nutshell, I am wed to a woman the more modest of whose habits is to wash down her breakfast croissants with Moët & Chandon. And I wouldn't have her any other way.

I grip the steering wheel with hands encased in leather driving gloves and rivet my eyes to the road. A wave of depression sweeps over me. We need a change of scene, I tell myself once again, a gust of fresh air in our lives. New York and our circle of decorative friends and cycle of syba-

ritic activities have been losing luster lately. I feel smothered. I wish it were possible for Nicole and me to break the
pattern and make a fresh start somewhere—not in a primitive arcadia, by any means—but in beautiful and luxurious
surroundings like Biarritz or Rio that are not too remote
from civilized pleasures. I don't kid myself that my acting
career is essential to my contentment. Even though I follow
a glamorous calling, I have always been (sadly, perhaps)
among the majority for whom one's occupation is a means
to an end rather than an end in itself. Maybe that's why I'm
such a rotten actor. Well, not rotten, really, not rotten to
the core (I have managed to develop some technical prow-
ess over the years), just uninspired, soulless. What I really
need is a big fat legacy of some sort.

Chooging my vintage horn at a slow driver, I frown
sourly at the thought of a legacy. I recall that I started off in
life with a modest trust fund from my father and that I
managed to piss it away in five or six years. I'm glad that my
father did not live to see me squander all that money, for it
would have wounded him deeply. The old coot was always
generous with me. In fact, much too generous. He and
mother spoiled me rotten. They seemed to be trying to
atone for some misty past injustice. Maybe it had to do
with my being adopted. I never really fathomed it.

There it is again—the recurring feeling of incomplete-
ness, of being only half a person. The feeling—strong, inef-
fable—eddies over me time after time. It puzzles me.
Maybe everyone has moments when he or she feels this
way, a sense of primal attachment to *otherness*, but I rather
believe that my experience is rare, if not unique.

Inadvertently, incorrigibly, I again gaze at my reflection
in the mirror and I wonder from whom I inherited this
finely sculpted face and beautiful coloring. My adoptive
father had a craggy and coarse face and no physical grace
whatsoever. My adoptive mother, while no great beauty,

had at least a hint of birdlike prettiness. They told me little of my real origins and I never felt compelled to press them on the matter.

It suddenly occurs to me that I'm out of beer, so I pull over and park near a fire hydrant in front of one of those Korean grocery markets that are now everywhere in Manhattan. I dash inside, hoping to complete the transaction before getting a parking ticket. I hurry to the freezer in the rear of the store and select a six-pack of Foster's. On the way to the cash register I grab a *baguette* of French bread, an avocado and a bunch of cut violets for Nicole. I curse under my breath to see a long line of customers waiting at the check-out counter but I fall in behind them, nervously eyeing my car. Soon I am inspecting the shapely calves and rear end of the woman in front of me, an ash-blond Greenwich Villager laden with oranges and bananas. My gaze is frank, my admiration unveiled. She smiles at me. Years of success with the opposite sex have cured me of the common male habit of covert lechery.

My eyes trace the swell of her hips. Rather voluptuous, much more fleshy than my slim and muscular Nicole. I am suddenly even more anxious to get home to her.

Outside, I note with relief that no slip of paper is stuck under the windshield wiper. A shade of annoyance crosses my face as I observe that the loose change I kept in the compartment near the gear shift has been pilfered. With a small sigh I count myself lucky that whoever did it hadn't damaged anything. I paid only a very small price for leaving an unattended convertible with the top down on a New York City street. I place the grocery bag on the passenger seat, slide behind the steering wheel and drive off, my thoughts still occupied by Nicole, my selfish, hedonistic, impossible, adorable Nicole.

She haunts me like a witch, thrills me like a succubus,

pampers me like a houri, exasperates me like a coltish child. I can't live without her.

At Bond Street I hit a traffic snarl caused by motorists rubbernecking at something, another act in the eternal side-show staged on the calico streets of this city. I finally see what all the fuss is about. This one's a pip, even for New York. A wino, stark naked except for an aviator cap and goggles, is dancing in the middle of the street. Even jaded Manhattanites pause to gape at this one. Men holler encouragement, girls titter behind their hands. A large crowd has gathered to ogle this dodo's flight over Broadway. I thump the horn with the heel of my hand. I have no interest in this comic opera. I just want to get home.

I finally maneuver the car through the tieup and go two more blocks until I hit a red light at Houston Street. Here derelicts and hustlers usually try to coax tips from motorists for smearing windshields with dirty rags. To avoid them if possible, I always try to beat the light at this corner. No such luck this time. I would have run the light except for a slowpoke old dame directly in front of me driving a rusty beige VW beetle. Sure enough, as soon as I jam on the brakes, a bum brandishing a rag heads for my car. I look away in disgust. It's hard to avoid these characters, especially when you're driving a convertible. If you try to wave them off, they usually pretend not to notice and advance anyway, stolid and mute like zombies.

A man's hand clutching a soiled blue polka-dot bandanna appears before my sorrowful eyes. I try not to look at him but I catch glimpses anyhow. He is dressed in a ragged camouflage fatigue jacket and baggy blue jeans. Under the grime his long matted hair is blondish. He swipes at the windshield in an insolent, half-hearted way, spreading fly flecks and soot.

I drum on the steering wheel. The wait for the light to

turn green seems interminable. The hand relentlessly wipes the windshield.

Arching my back and lifting my rear end from the seat, I dig into my pockets for a dollar bill to give him. I have only a fiver but I decide on a sudden impulse to give it to him anyhow. As I hand him the money something compels me to examine his face more closely.

At first, none of the subtleties of his features register, none of the elements that make up the soul. I see merely the obvious external things, the stubble of the beard, the grime in the crevices of the skin and, especially, the crop of ugly fever blisters on his cheeks and forehead.

Then, all of a sudden, under the blatancies, I see the real face beneath the facade of suffering and self-abuse. My heart leaps to my throat.

The light changes to green. I press on the gas pedal and drive off, a glazed expression on my face. I am practically numb. I change gears, guide the steering wheel, work clutch, brake and pedal, all in mindless mechanical fashion. The car heads downtown and goes right on Prince Street. I have received a shock to my system but I am absolutely certain of what I saw. It was no illusion, no figment. I know what I saw.

The face of the derelict beneath the tangled beard and grime, beneath the pallid complexion and fever sores, beneath the mask of hopelessness and resentment, was identical to my own.

Identical.

CHAPTER 2

My origins are foggy but I know this much: I was born out of wedlock somewhere near Dover, Delaware. I have, unlike most people, uncannily early primal memories as if I somehow missed my turn at the lethean stream. My memories date back to infancy. I can see even now in my mind's lens a patch of blue sky filled with scudding clouds and flying mastodons from the nearby air cargo terminal. Am I lying on my back in a cradle, crib or bassinet? I hear the trilling of a bird and mingled with this sound a strange idiolalic babble. I am not alone; of this I am certain. I am instinctively certain that I was also not alone when I made the traumatic journey down the dark passageway and into the glare of this odd world of the sun.

Soon came the *separation*. After the separation I have always felt, as I mentioned earlier, incomplete.

I was adopted by Jeremiah Beck and his wife Sally. My adoptive father was a reserve Air Force colonel who later inherited his father's partnership in an investment banking firm. Sally Beck was barren. I was christened Evan Beck and raised in comfortable circumstances in Scarsdale, New York. I was a gorgeous child and they coddled me like a prince. Every day was Christmas. I chose my own nannies, ruled the household. My father had a shed built in the back yard just to house my collection of bicycles, scooters, wagons and other vehicular toys. I had my own horse, Pal, stabled at a nearby riding academy.

I attended private schools, of course. In high school I excelled in football and basketball and became captain of the swim team. I even played polo. I did moderately well in my studies, even though I paid scant attention to them. In my sophomore year I discovered that I had a talent for drawing, sketching and, later, painting. The discovery tapped a spate of new feelings in me and gave me great satisfaction. In the world of line and color I felt less incomplete. But having been pampered made me indolent and I never worked hard enough to cultivate this talent to the fullest. I often regret it. I'm fairly certain that I would have made a better painter than actor. Be that as it may . . .

With the girls I made out like a bandit. Since even before I reached puberty they threw themselves at my feet. I had the classic experiences (an *au pair* seduced me when I was thirteen). There were a few notable exceptions to this slavish devotion by females (e.g., Nicole!), but for the most part I could pick and choose like a sultan. Of course this facility had the natural effect of somewhat jading my tastes.

Since traditional academic studies did not interest me, I spurned my father's offer to get me into Cornell (his alma mater) and enrolled instead at NYU where I had vague ideas of studying filmmaking but where I actually majored in bar-hopping, skirt-chasing and reefer-rolling. At the after-hours joints I met a number of casting directors and my Don Juan looks opened plenty of doors. Soon I was getting modeling jobs and bit parts in plays and movies. I never bothered to finish college. Thus was launched my mediocre acting career, now in its sunset.

These reflections and memories occupy me as I operate the freight elevator, ascending to the top floor of our loft apartment building on Mercer Street. Introspection is not my strong suit. But the encounter with my alter ego on Houston Street has revived old questions and speculations about my origins.

I step into the apartment, riffling through a stack of mail. "Niki," I shout, my voice echoing across the huge space. I can't wait to tell her about it. No answer. I suddenly remember that she spends Tuesday evenings with her body-building instructor, improving her definition. The sessions with André Kaplan seem to be taking longer and longer lately. If he weren't such a muscle-bound pinhead I might be jealous. Nicole's a funny kid, I reflect, shaking my head. She builds her body up with barbells and tears it down with dissolute living.

I stride across the glossy oak floor to the kitchen area, remove a can of beer from the plastic holder and put the rest in the fridge. I leave the bread and avocado on the butcher block counter and arrange the flowers in a ceramic vase that I fill with tap water. I pop open the beer and take a long slug straight from the can.

I walk over to the studio on the east end of the loft space. It is a bright room with two large skylights and it is filled with paint, tools and massive canvases, some empty, some completed, some half-finished, embodiments of irresolution and doubt, splotches of courage in color. My medium is traditional—oils—and my technique is idiosyncratic and hard to classify, sometimes representational, sometimes not.

I sip beer and study a work-in-progress, an abstract piece dominated by dark blue colors and chaotic forms. I tilt my head, squint, bite my lip, make guttural sounds. Do I like it? Should I finish it? I sigh. I know I'm a fairly good painter but I'm not sure how good. I have no formal training. I've never shown my work to a qualified judge. By nature I am an autodidact and I have read widely and well in many areas, including the visual arts, but it's hard to be objective about one's own work. I frown, lean the canvas gingerly against the wall, and leave the room.

The stack of mail sits ominously on the end table near my easy chair by the huge double-hung windows overlooking Greene Street. No more procrastinating. I settle into the leather chair and inspect the correspondence by the light of the druggist lamp that Nicole bought from a haggling old Lebanese on Atlantic Avenue in Brooklyn. The beer can stands on the table at my left elbow. I take another swig and sigh again. The letter carrier has brought nothing but junk mail and dunning letters. I find one meager residual check from a TV commercial. Worries about impending financial disaster have distracted me momentarily from the remarkable encounter that has occupied my thoughts since I saw him. I see with a special twinge that one of the letters bears the return address of the bank that holds the mortgage on the beach house. I don't even have to open it. We're three months in arrears and I'm certain that they are threatening legal action. Immediately I make a mental computation of our resources to see if I can pay them a piece without removing essential ballast from another end of the hold. It's no dice. We're hopelessly overextended, I conclude. We might have to liquidate something. But what? The loft? Not feasible. We both need a home base in Manhattan for our various activities, both social and professional. We need the jeep and the car too, not that they would provide enough to get us out of this jam anyhow.

Maybe we could hit up somebody for a loan—a temporary solution. Nicole might ask her mother for a few grand. After all it's my wife's drug habit and other costly appetites and avocations that put us into this hole in the first place. Of course, the thought of even broaching the subject to her makes me shudder. The letter from the bank seems to sear my fingertips. I palm it like a conjurer but it doesn't disappear.

Of course, we could sell the beach house in Davis Park but that would devastate both of us. We made love for the first time in the swimming pool there. And how would we escape the hustle and bustle of Manhattan? No, it's unrealistic to think that either of us, self-indulgent epicures that we are, is capable of any real belt-tightening. I'll just have to come up with a way of making some money.

Easier said than done. I wish I could cash in the life insurance policy my father bequeathed to me for the benefit of his nonexistent grandchildren. It's worth a million-and-a-half. The only way I can collect on it is to drop dead. Next idea?

I have finished the beer. I dearly need another.

By the time I have returned from the refrigerator, sunk into the chair and popped open another can, I have also rejected a few more solutions on my mental checklist, such as knocking off liquor stores, going into the white slavery business or offering my services as a hit man. My thoughts drift. The beer is making me drowsy. I float into a shuddery nap.

An hour later the wall phone in the kitchen rings. I leap from the chair, shake off the cobwebs and stumble over to it.

"Hullo."

Histrionic heavy breathing on the other end.

"Niki, is that you?"

"How are you dressed?" she asks in a mock-throaty voice.

"Cut it out, Nik. What time is it? Where the hell are you?"

"In bikinis or boxers? What color? Describe the stitching on the crotch. Oh, please!"

"I am dressed in gloom, sweetheart. Come home."

Her voice becomes normal. I hear a babble of voices and socializing in the background. She's obviously calling from a joint.

"I stopped in at Fanelli's for a salad," she says. "Care to join me?"

"Not really." I yawn with ostentation. "I repeat, what time is it?"

"Early. Ten-thirty. Why ask me? Why don't you just look at the clock over the elevator?"

"Can't see that far. I'm in my chair."

"You, my love, are getting old and decrepit."

"Forty's not old. This loft is two thousand square feet big."

"Ah, but you used to be able to see the wall clock from your chair."

I'm stumped. "Forty's not old," I repeat petulantly.

"Just think," she says in a similar chord, "at forty Mozart was already dead for five years."

I frown at the phone. "What the hell's that supposed to mean?"

She laughs over the din of the restaurant. "Nothing, *mon amour*. I'll come right home."

"Good. And shake your ass. I have something rather re-markable to tell you."

"What? I hate mysteries, you know that."

"I can't tell you over the phone. Hurry home."

"Be there in a flash, sweet potato."

I hang up, depressed. I try again to focus on the wall clock face but it's a smudge. Maybe I am old, I reflect. Old, sunk in debt and at the end of my professional tether. A burnt-out case. I feel sorry for myself.

Then suddenly I think about my double on Houston

Street and I feel a little sheepish about wallowing in self-pity. He is really a burnt-out case and I don't want to tempt the fates by losing my sense of proportion.

I sit in the armchair and wait for her to come home. I yawn again and glance at the yellowing leaves of a ficus tree standing by the three steps leading to the fire escape that we use as a terrace garden, filling it with potted geraniums, petunias and trailing ivy. I now remember fragments of the dream I had during the nap. It is a recurrent dream, morbid and paradoxically pleasurable. I dreamed of attending my own funeral.

CHAPTER 3

The buzzer sounds and I go down in the freight elevator to get her. As I manipulate the lever I reflect that if she routinely would walk up the four flights she might not need to take so many bodybuilding lessons and aerobics classes to stay in shape. We might save a little money. Then I wonder, is jealousy of André surfacing? Nah. Why should I worry about a primping pansy in spandex?

The elevator groans. Only New Yorkers would pay astronomical prices for apartments where you have to serve as your own elevator operator and take out your own garbage. Only New Yorkers would live in converted factories in neighborhoods where you have to dodge trucks and climb over loading platforms to walk the dog. Only New Yorkers would tend geraniums and marigolds on fire escapes above the stench of rotting garbage. And the real estate brokers tag it luxury living. With an ironic wag of the head, I watch the paint-blistered exterior walls of my neighbors' apartments rise before me as the elevator descends.

The cab hits the ground floor with a thud. I release the

lever. I slide back the metal grate and shoulder open the heavy door, revealing a vision in olive green tweed who is my wife, Nicole Roche Beck.

After five years of marriage her beauty still works its magic on me. Though slim and small she paradoxically has a larger-than-life physical presence. What accounts for it? Grace of movement, pride of bearing, that elusive something called charisma? Hard to say. What made Menelaus throw down his sword before the daughter of a swan? A tilt of Nicole's well-formed head gives me more shivers than the sashays of a hundred women. The head is crowned by a thatch of tightly-curled chestnut hair and the face enlivened by a pair of large sparkling green eyes made even more vivid by the burnished brown tone of her complexion.

With a courtly hand flourish I usher her into the elevator.

"Thanks, Lochinvar," she says brightly and steps inside the cab.

I mumble hello.

With an arch of her eyebrow she studies my gloomy face. "Something eating you?"

I shake my head. "Not really."

"That means yes," she says in a sage, wifely tone.

I work the lever and the elevator groans again. "I'm just glad you're home." I look directly at her and she gives me a routine smile. She's wearing pink lipstick, freshly applied.

Inside the loft she mixes herself a Pimm and seltzer, kicks off her shoes and drapes herself on the couch. She rattles on about this and that, in an upbeat mood—a natural high, I'm pretty certain.

She notices the flowers and the avocado on the countertop. "For me? How sweet!" She goes over to the kitchen, primps the violets and buries her nose in them. Then she asks idly, "How did the powwow with Mitch go?"

I fidget in the armchair and shrug, studying my laced fingers.

"Not so good, huh?"

"Inconclusive."

"Meaning?"

"He didn't have any major ideas about jump-starting my career. But he says not to worry, I'll be okay. Just the doldrums, etcetera."

"You didn't believe him."

I shake my head and raise my eyes from my manicured fingers to her fine-boned face. She's thirty, a flower in full bloom. She looks much younger and has the muscle tone of a teenager. She sits in the chair opposite me, crosses her slim tan legs and holds the drink chin high, her pinky pointing skyward.

"You'll get back on your feet," she says in a dull tone that lacks conviction. "With your dynamite looks."

"Yeah? Sometimes dynamite blows up in your face."

"Oh pooh." She inspects the frost of condensation on her ice-filled glass.

I feel on the verge of tears.

Now she spots the stack of bills on the table next to me. "Uh-oh," she says, putting down the drink and standing up. "Now I know what brought on this foul mood." She walks over to the window, deliberately averting her gaze from the bills. "It's a chilly night," she says, shuddering slightly.

I frown, my patience a little frayed by her meadowlarking attitude. "We've got to do something," I declare.

Lines of worry rut her burnished brow. "We?" she asks.

That's one of the things I love about her. She wears her selfishness like the Congressional Medal of Honor.

"The well's running dry, sweetheart."

"Couldn't you sell some stocks?"

Rubbing my lightly stubbled chin I consider this suggestion. It would tide us over for a few months, I suppose. "I guess so. I hesitate, though. I hate to use up our last life preserver."

She grunts, noncommittal.

"We could sell the loft," I venture.

"I will not be reduced to squalor."

I look around. "Some people would consider *this* squalor."

She ignores the remark, sipping Pimm. I can see her lips forming a remark, then hesitating. Finally she says it: "I know what you want. You want me to put the bite on *Maman.*"

"I don't know if I want that," I reply honestly. "But I must admit that the thought crossed my mind."

She turns away from the window, hands on her hips. "And entered a little black hole where it soon disappeared, I trust, like all ill-considered notions. How could I possibly borrow money from that witch when we're barely on speaking terms?"

I look up with a trace of annoyance. "You spoke to her just two days ago."

She whirls back to the window, not condescending to face me. "Spoke? We didn't speak. We hissed and barked and growled and roared and whinnied and bayed and blustered and howled and bleated and brayed and snarled." She catches her breath after this virtuoso verbal performance. "We made a lot of sounds, none of which would qualify as civilized speech."

"Oh, come on. You guys are closer than you let on."

She ponders this assertion with a mock-serious expression. Then she says, "I suppose you could say that Dr. Roche and I are close in the same sense that *matador* and *toro*, Arab and Jew, mongoose and serpent are close. We share the intimacy of sworn enemies."

"How can you talk about your own mother that way? Boy, your father must have done a job on you!"

She replies, spacing the words, "Shut. Up." Then she crosses the room to refill her drink.

I grow conciliatory. "Sorry, honey. Bring me another beer?"

"Tut, tut. You don't want to develop a beer belly, do you? Not in your line of work."

A wounded look crosses my face. "I don't need to worry. I'm active. I play squash and basketball. I swim laps in the pool."

"Only when we're at the beach house."

"Please get me the beer," I insist. "My tummy's as tight as a drum." I should know. I inspect my naked body in a full-length mirror at least twice a day. But in a curious way I would welcome the slackening effects of age. It would be a relief to finally desert the ramparts, slouch before an easel and paints, bow to the gods of indolence.

I fall silent and submit to a funky mood. An icy wind whistles through the drafty windows, a hint of winter in the October air. I reflect how much I love summer, season of fruition. I like it much better than spring which merely promises what summer delivers. No, Mr. Eliot, July is the cruelest month.

I gaze at my wife as she returns from the kitchen. Nicole is an estival type of woman—vibrant, colorful, blooming, juicy. She holds the frosty beer can in front of my staring eyes.

"Let's go to the house," I suddenly suggest. I take the beer from her hand.

"But it's already October."

"The weather's still good." I rub my hands together. "Except for tonight. Let's try to prolong the summer."

She hesitates. "I don't know."

"Come on. The weatherman predicts a stretch of balmy weather. There's nothing for us to do here."

"I have my bodybuilding class. And other things."

"Throw your barbells in the jeep."

She bites her lower lip. "Okay." She saunters over to the stereo and sticks in a reggae tape. Her hips undulate to the music. I watch her in the mirrors that line a row of closets on the opposite wall. Then my gaze shifts to the image of myself, slouched in the chair. I regard the reflection for a few minutes and am suddenly struck by the notion that it is not my image I am seeing, and not quite that of another person either, but the rippled form of an undine who lives in the depths of the glass and somehow has a personal claim on my soul. The unpleasant subject of our money problems has distracted me from telling her about my double.

On an impulse, I say to Nicole, "Did I ever tell you I was born a twin?"

Nicole stops swaying to the music and turns to face me. "No. Were you?"

I nod. "For as far back as I could remember I always felt this intimate connection to another person. I once asked my parents about it. They told me that my twin died at birth along with my natural mother. But I never believed them."

"Why not?"

I hunch my shoulders and shake my head. "I don't know. No logical reason, really. It was a perfectly plausible story. But I had a gut feeling. A very strong one. It was as if I was incomplete all by myself and that somewhere on this planet walked my brother—more than a brother, almost another self." I roll the beer around my tongue and stare into the distance. "Funny, the idea of him was both threatening and comforting. It was like a threat to my identity, my individuality. The world wasn't big enough for two of me. Maybe he would come out of the blue some day and take what is rightfully mine. Then again it was solacing to think that I had a soul mate somewhere."

"A womb mate," she puns. "Was he identical or fraternal?"

"My parents didn't know. I know for certain. I think I always knew. He is my identical twin." I give her a look of dark significance.

She looks skeptical. "How can you be so sure?"

I gaze back at my reflection in the mirror. "Because I saw him. Earlier this evening."

CHAPTER 4

*L*ater Nicole takes a shower while I try to read the newspaper. I can't concentrate. I feel pleased we are spending a night at home for once, like two domestic cats, instead of being caught up in the social maelstrom of cocktail parties and gallery openings. We should do this more often.

The night ripens. Through the window I see a lemony moon, almost full, in the eastern sky. I listen to the spatter of shower water and contemplate Nicole's reaction to the news that I have seen my double. Naturally she was doubtful that he was my twin. Lots of people look alike, she said in effect, brushing the subject aside. But I'm still thoroughly convinced that I saw my twin brother. I've read accounts of twins being separated at birth and then being reunited and have speculated (hoped? suspected?) that someday it might happen to me too. What I didn't expect is that he would turn out to be a gutter rat wiping windshields on Houston Street. It evoked disturbing thoughts of a there-but-for-the-grace-of-God variety and a guilty pleasure as well. The memory of him gives me gooseflesh.

I feel a pang of hunger and I put down the unread newspaper and head for the kitchen, having decided to surprise Nicole with a midnight snack when she gets out of the shower. I poke inside the refrigerator and my hands emerge carrying lettuce, lemon juice and Canadian bacon. I put these items next to the French bread and avocado on the butcher block counter. I feel a minor key excitement about preparing this food for Nicole. I am, I know, a pretty selfish and callous person in most respects. Not when it comes to her, though. She herself is a hard-hearted Hannah but for some reason she has a thawing effect on me. Go figure.

Mooning a little bit, I imagine her naked in the shower as I begin to peel the avocado, always a slippery operation.

The cut on my right index finger is deep and clean. Fighting nausea I shout over the sound of running shower water, "Niki-i-i!"

At first she doesn't hear me. I call to her again in a louder voice. With a squeak of plumbing the shower is turned off.

"Did you say something?"

"Come quickly. I cut myself."

Soon she pads out of the bathroom drenched and naked, carrying a handful of items from the medicine cabinet. Her face conveys a cool determination, her movements measured efficiency. She is good in emergencies and, since her mother is a doctor, knows exactly what to do. In very few minutes the wound is clean, disinfected and expertly bandaged.

"Now how the hell did that happen?"

I look sheepish. "I was fixing us a midnight snack. I know how much you like avocado salad."

"Garnished with finger?"

My glance sweeps over her. Her hair is dewy and ringletted with humidity. Her breasts gleam like washed fruit. She leans coquettishly on the counter. "How about that snack?" she asks.

I pick up the knife and go back to what I was doing while she returns to the bathroom. When she comes back she's still naked and is toweling her hair. With her back toward me she stands on her tiptoes and makes a turban of the towel, wrapping it around her head. Her ass is round and satiny.

"You should have been a doctor too," I remark, arranging the avocado slices on a stoneware plate and garnishing them with bacon I have cooked in the microwave.

"No, thanks," she says, facing me with a sardonic frown. "The bitch always wanted me to, though."

"You have a knack for it."

"I'm perfectly content with the life of an empty-headed and dissolute playgirl. Hurry up with that food. I'm suddenly famished." She rolls a joint and begins to smoke it.

We eat in silence, soft music on the tape deck. She has donned an Oriental silk kimono. Her showered skin glows and her green eyes glint like polished jade. She drinks a glass of Hermitage with the salad.

Before long, leaving the mess for our housekeeper, Sophie, to clean up in the morning, we go to bed and make love. As usual, our lovemaking is a mixture of expertise and abandon, the playful juncture of two narcissists with good bodies and wide experience. In the susurrant aftermath she smokes another joint and I stare at the ceiling.

"I love you, Nicole," I say out of nowhere.

"Me too," she says abstractedly, watching the smoke climb.

"You love you too?"

"You know what I mean."

The scent of marijuana reaches me. "I know."

She asks, "Are you going to sell the stock?"

I sigh for the demise of the serene mood we were enjoying. "I guess so."

She snuggles gratefully into the cavity of my chest and

her finger traces the muscles of my abdomen. She says, "I wonder what it would be like."

"What would what be like?"

"To have you and your so-called twin brother in bed at the same time."

"You have a nasty imagination."

"Yes I do." She watches the smoke curl upward. "Hey, I just got another wild idea."

"Which is . . . ?"

"It's the answer to our financial problems. Listen—we pick up this bum who's your spitting image. We clean him up and bump him off. Then we pretend the body's you, collect on your life insurance and hightail it for South America or Capetown or someplace like that. We could be sitting pretty for the rest of our lives."

"On second thought you should not be a doctor." I give a mock shudder. "Agatha Creepy."

"He's just a bum, a derelict, a nobody, a drain on society. Who would miss him? We'd be putting him out of his misery."

I examine her face behind the shadows. "You're not serious, are you?"

"Half-serious."

I lie back on the pillow, locking my hands behind my head. "That must be powerful stuff you're smoking."

"Yeah. My head's a fantasy factory."

"Anyhow," I remark in a curious key of regret, "I'll probably never see him again."

"Probably not," she mumbles into the pillow, curling her lovely body into a fetal position. Soon her breathing is shallow and even.

I lie awake staring at the embossed tin ceiling, lost in thought. My cut finger throbs slightly and I remember the sight of my blood.

But I do see him again three days later as I am driving home from a visit uptown to my stockbroker. He stands on the island of concrete where Houston Street intersects Broadway. As I drive past in the Jaguar I notice that he has come up in the world. Instead of carrying a soiled rag he now carries a red plastic pail filled with soap and water and a squeegee. He is still dressed in the camouflage jacket and blue jeans. The light is green and I drive past.

My pulse races. My second look at him has only served to confirm the first impression that, under the ravages of poverty and alcoholism and God knows what other deficiencies, he looks exactly like me. I suppose he is a regular fixture on this corner, at least until the weather gets too raw. I can't wait to tell Nicole about it. I press down on the gas pedal.

We walk the few blocks back to Houston Street. Nicole's tongue is literally in her cheek. I want to observe him at closer range and in a leisurely way.

We approach Houston from Wooster Street and walk east in the twilight toward Broadway. The wind wails at our backs, bringing the scent of the river and impending rain. My heart beats quickly. Dim memories of a warm climate and a soft presence loom in my mind.

We reach the southeast intersection and stop. My eyes scan the area for him, a scarecrow figure in olive drab. I see cars halted in the westbound lane of Houston Street. Then I survey the other side of the street in front of the gas station.

No sign of him. I look up. A sparrow struggles across the wide gray sky.

"He's gone," I say gloomily.

Nicole gives me an ironic sidelong glance.

"He was here just ten minutes ago," I protest.

"I believe you. I believe you." She stands on the pavement, the wind flapping her short cotton skirt against bronze legs. The eyes of male passersby turn to her appraisingly. The sun sinks at her back.

I point to the pedestrian island. "He was standing right there," I say.

She shrugs. "Maybe he got run over."

I look irritated and disappointed. "Let's go home," I suggest.

As I start to turn around I catch sight of him emerging from a clutch of people gathered near the roadside fruit and vegetable stand on the east side of the street. He is peeling an orange. Hanging from the crook of his elbow is the pail of water and the squeegee. I feel an odd surge of jubilation.

"There he is!" I exclaim, pointing my finger. He shambles across the street. I notice that he is as tall as I but that he carries himself in a stoop-shouldered and vanquished way. Relieved of his psychic and physical burdens his posture and gait, I imagine, would have the same jauntiness as mine.

"Who? Where?" She still sounds skeptical. I put my arms around her shoulders and steer her toward the fruit stand. Her eyes search the sidewalk scene, flicking over the assortment of Spanglish wholesale sportswear stores and lunch counters, past the array of vendors in this Occidental souk, their wares set up on bridge tables and beneath beach umbrellas—cheap watches, shoes, clothes, sunglasses, transistor batteries, schlock jewelry, earrings, cosmetics, tube socks, windup toys and nylon tote bags.

"I still don't see him."

I gently place my hand on her chin and swivel her head in his direction. "The guy in the camouflage jacket crossing the street and eating an orange."

He darts through traffic and reaches the other side. He leans against a post of the subway entrance and hungrily devours the fruit. "That guy?" she says. "He doesn't look like you."

"Maybe not from this distance. But, take my word for it, you've got to see him up close."

Her shiny brown face looks determined. "Well, you wait right here and I'll do just that." She steps off on one foot, then turns back. "Let me have some change," she says.

I fish two quarters from my pocket. "What are you going to do?"

"He's a beggar, isn't he? Watch."

She strides across the street, swaying her hips, muscles rippling in her tapered calves; she resembles a thoroughbred animal, tail sashaying.

He now stands under the Amoco sign. He has finished the orange and swishes the water in the pail with the squeegee, obviously preparing to wash a few more windshields. He seems startled at the approach of a very pretty woman handing him change without having been asked. They look at each other briefly. He takes the money with a sullen nod of thanks and she turns on her heel and walks off.

"So?" I say when she returns, unable to conceal my excitement. Her face is indecipherable, a blank. But soon she nods her head.

"Am I right?" I ask, seeking stronger confirmation.

"Castor and Pollux . . ." she says, nodding vigorously now.

"Didn't I tell you?"

"Romulus and Remus . . ."

"Yes, yes, yes . . ."

"Jacob and Esau . . ."

"Heckle and Jeckle," I echo in the prevailing spirit.

"Evan Beck and the derelict of Houston Street." She glances wonderingly at him as he shuffles into the street to wipe a windshield. "Under all the dreck, your ever-lovin' clone. It's really awesome."

Back at the loft I brew herbal tea that we sip in silence before a cozy crackling fire we have built in the cast-iron wood-burning stove in the kitchen. She drinks tea sweetened with honey and frowns reflectively over a crockery mug, the sharp planes of her heart-shaped face accented by the firelight.

"Something wrong?" I ask.

She shakes her head, sips tea. I can see the flames leaping in her sea-green eyes. Or are they poison-bottle green? "What are you hatching?" I ask in a tone that mingles admiration and reproof.

Her lips part, petals in a belladonna smile. "Nothing," she says. "Nothing."

I am not convinced.

The next evening I'm waiting for Niki in the twilight under the Washington Square arch, our rendezvous for a movie date. It's convenient. *My Man Godfrey* is showing at a revival house in the East Village and Nicole's shrink rents space for his couch just up the block on Fifth Avenue. As I wait, leaning against the stone pedestal of the monument, I am approached by three panhandlers and two loose joint peddlers whose wares I politely decline.

The appearance of the panhandlers here under the shedding trees has made me think again about my twin brother, or whoever he is. Of course I have not been able to get him out of my mind. I know I should do something about his existence, befriend him or help him out or at least in some fashion satisfy my curiosity about him and our relationship. But for some reason I am paralyzed. What accounts for this reticence or fear or whatever? I'm not at all sure.

I check my wrist watch. She's only ten minutes late so I calculate that I have at least another ten minutes to wait. We won't be late for the movie because I have a standing policy of pushing the clock back a half hour and lying to her about when an event begins. I gaze idly at the dog walkers, joggers and college girls. It's a breezy but mild evening, very pleasant.

I reflect on another obsession that has somewhat distracted me from thinking about my double—our financial straits. A man from the bank that holds the mortgage on the beach house called me today on the phone. He was very nasty. I dread telling Nicole about it. Dirty little details such as decimal points and due dates give her hives and mar her peaches and cream complexion.

Speak of the Devil's daughter here she is, flouncing down Fifth, a vision in leather and suede, a luxury liner who leaves swirling male heads in her wake.

She pecks me on the mouth. "Hullo, plumcake, sorry I'm late."

I appraise her miniskirt. "Hello, gorgeous."

"Window shopping, you know how I am. Completely lost track of time. Let's grab a cab." She tippy-toes on spiked heels, peering at traffic, and her skirt hitches up another inch.

We hail a cab going east on Washington Square North. She climbs in first, flashing beige legs. Once inside the cab we kiss for real and her tongue worms all over my mouth, improving my mood. Then she draws away and touches up her lipstick.

"What's new, heartthrob?" she asks.

"Plenty."

"I don't like the sound of that." With a twist she closes up the lipstick and puts it into her handbag, simultaneously rooting for her cigarettes.

I tell her all about the call from the bank. She seems eminently bored.

She pounds the cigarette against the back of her hand to pack the tobacco tight. "Can't you sell the stock?" she asks.

"I discussed the idea with Modesto yesterday. He's

against it. He says it's a bad time to unload now. We'll take a shellacking."

"When does the bank want the money?"

"Yesterday."

She hesitates, then suggests, "Why don't you sell the Fletcher Martin? It ought to bring in a nice piece of change, enough to hold the bank at bay for a while anyhow."

"It's only my favorite painting," I say with a twisted mouth.

"Well I think it's hideous. Of course you know that already." She lights the cigarette.

"It will only increase in value as the years pass," I observe.

"Please, Madam," the cab driver breaks in. "No smoking."

I glance at him for the first time. He's a cocoa-skinned East Indian.

"I beg your pardon?" she says in the haughtiest tone she can muster.

He jabs with his finger at a red-lettered sign he has placed on the dashboard. "No smoking, if you please."

"Well fuck you, Gunga Din," she says, taking a deep drag on the cigarette and blowing out great plumes of smoke.

"Madam, I have a condition," he pleads.

"You're telling me," she says acidly.

"Please, Niki," I say.

Her eyes flash at me. "Forget it, darling," she says. "No coolie's going to tell me when or where to pollute my lungs."

The driver sets his mouth and applies the brakes. He says, "I vill have to ahsk you to get out of the taxi."

"Niki," I beg. "We're almost there."

Suddenly she hurls the cigarette out of the open window. "Okay," she mutters to me. "I'll fix his wagon."

My expression darkens because I know what she means.

She turns to me and says, "And if you tip him one nickle I'll divorce you." She rummages in her bag again and takes out a plastic vial containing yellow liquid that she always carries with her for just such occasions.

I sigh deeply.

When we reach our destination I hold open the taxi door for her.

Still seated, she pulls the stopper out of the vial and gives the driver a burlesque smile. "Have a nice day," she says, pouring the piss over the back seat and getting out of the cab.

My wife is not a dull person. During the movie she insists on doing the popcorn trick—cutting a hole in the bottom of a popcorn box, placing it on my lap and giving me a hand job. I object only feebly and soon I am spurting semen over her salty hand while I listen to Carole Lombard's whine. The seeds are sown.

Afterwards we have hamburgers at Phoebe's.

I stare at the quadrangle of less-faded paint on the wall where the Fletcher Martin used to hang. The art dealer rooked me, of course, but the few grand that we got will keep the hyenas from the door for about another month or so. Then what, I wonder?

Nicole is lounging beside me on the couch, reading a fashion magazine. Her calf rests on my shoulder and her big toe caresses my cheek.

"We'd better fire Sophie," I say.

Without blinking, her eyes continue to scan the page. "Not on your life." Tapping four fingers on her mouth, she yawns.

I'm about to protest but I give up the idea. The robe she wears has parted, giving me a vista of long legs and cleft valley. "It hurt to part with that painting," I observe with a pout.

She looks at me and forms a moue of mock sympathy. "I know, dear heart. You're a very big person and I'm a selfish prima donna. But Sophie stays or I go."

"You mean it too."

"I always say what I mean and mean what I say. You know that."

"I know that."

"I'm dependable." She smiles and throws the magazine on the cocktail table. She rises and her slender fingers reach across for an ivory cigarette box. She flips it open and extracts a reefer.

I sigh. "I can't keep selling paintings. I don't have any more that are worth anything."

She lights up. Her expression is unconcerned. "I know," she says. "We have to find a permanent, long-term solution to our cash flow problems."

"Right."

"I've been doing some thinking."

"About?"

She leans back, her emerald eyes aglitter with a grim thought. "Your double," she says.

"My double?"

"Yes."

I stare into her eyes. I shake my head and say, "You can't be thinking what I think you're thinking. What you mentioned the other day was only a joke, wasn't it?"

She is draped across the sofa, a languorous Oriental queen without a care or conscience. She is Salome asking for a head. She fills her lungs with smoke, then watches wisps ascend to the tin ceiling. "Was it?" she asks.

"You're a witch, Niki. A witch without warts."

Her sandaled feet touch the floor and she leans forward on her bare kneecaps. "Listen to me, Evan," she says in a sugary voice. "It's the chance of a lifetime. Let's grab it."

"Witch, witch, witch."

With her right hand she makes a hexing motion. "Only bad witches are beautiful," she says, twisting Billie Burke's lines. "But I'm serious about this."

I give a slight shudder. "I know you are." I study her expression, the grim set of her silken mouth, the gloss in her eyes that is not merely reflected fire.

"We could easily befriend him," she says, "and take him into seclusion with us to Fire Island. We'll clean him up. Give him a steady supply of booze or whatever else he needs to keep him docile. We'll pamper him like a pasha. He won't know what hit him."

"Fattening the goose for liver paté." I put down the tea-cup and it clatters in the saucer.

"It could work, Evan. It could really work."

"I'm not really hearing this. It's a drug-related dream."

The fire highlights the pleasing geometry of her face, now impish and excited. "Think of it, Evan. One-and-a-half-million greenbacks. Wallow for a while like a pig in the thought of it. One-and-a-half-million. Plus all we can get from the sale of our apartment and the house and all the rest of our assets. Then Rio or Malaga. Sydney or Sardinia. We could spin out our lives like royalty. And you could paint to your heart's content and never have to make a cattle call again in your life."

"I don't go on cattle calls."

"The way your career is going you might have to start," she says, using the rapier.

I brood, glowering over the teacup. Her arguments are hitting home. Then, raising my voice, I say, "For God's sake he's my twin brother. A chick from the same fucking egg."

"We don't know that for sure."

I point to my gut. "I know it here."

She falls silent and her face darkens. "Euthanasia," she says. "Ever hear of euthanasia? You'd be doing your clone a favor." She stubs out the joint. "Besides I can't live in pinched circumstances, Evan. You know that."

"It will never work," I say, leaving the subject open, indicating that I have not completely rejected the idea. "How will we do it? Suppose he doesn't go along with us to Davis Park? There are so many imponderables."

She brightens, sensing that my resistance is weakening. "I'll take care of all the details. Just leave them to me. What do we have to lose by trying?"

I have a waking reverie about attending my own funeral, listening to my own eulogy. "What about me?" I ask. "Do I just disappear from the face of the earth?"

"Keep your passport. Go to France or wherever we designate. After the funeral and a decent interval I'll join you there. With all that money we can easily buy you a new identity and papers. It's foolproof."

She picks up an andiron and stokes the fire, letting her words sink in. Then she returns to the couch and drapes her arm around my slumped shoulders. "Listen, Evan. How many people get the chance to wipe the slate clean, to erase their lives and start from scratch? And not only with a clean slate, sweetheart, but also with about two million big ones to smooth the way?"

"And a guilty conscience."

"Oh pooh. Guilt is for the weak." Her fingers massage the nape of my neck. "Think of it, no more auditions for supercilious directors and casting agents. No more degrading offers for bit parts Off-Broadway. No more dim-witted producers offering you scripts about extraterrestrials and tragic AIDS victims. All you have to do is paint and commune with your soul like you always wanted to."

"How can I commune with my soul after I've sold it?" I look directly at her. She seems unmoved. I say, "Killing him would be like . . . like suicide."

"Yes. Except you can come back from the dead." She laughs.

"You make murder sound like an amusing little *divertissement.*"

She snuggles closer and her hand now kneads the flesh just above my kneecap. "Remember what I said before: he's just a down-at-the-heel derelict. What's he got to live for except a slow death? We'll be doing him a favor making it quick after giving him a great deal of pleasure."

The pupils of her eyes have narrowed to feline slits. She ruffles my hair. "You are, sweet husband, one hunk of man."

I peer into her smoky eyes and glimpse there, in the glow of the waning fire, my own reflection. And the witch begins to perform her magic.

CHAPTER 5

Naturally I refuse to go along with her outlandish plan. After all I'm not a total patsy. Even her threat to ditch me (it still echoes in my head: "I'll just pack my Guccis and say adieu") left me unswayed. But soon the straw comes that breaks my hump.

My beeper sounds during the tiebreaker in the final set at my tennis club.

"Gotta call my service," I tell Ken Boardman, my opponent.

"Finish first," he suggests.

"I'll be too distracted," I say, grabbing a towel and wiping my face. "I'll lose."

"Then you forfeit. The hour's nearly up."

"Okay," I say, impersonating a whining adolescent. "You win, you win. But it's a hollow victory." I make a dash for the pay phone by the drink machines outside the locker room.

It's good news for once. Mitch has landed me an audition for a second-lead running part in a private eye TV series being filmed in New York. The producer owes him a favor and I have the inside track. It would mean big money and a long-term contract. The audition is set for the following day.

I do very well. The casting director does not give me a simple "Thank you very much" (meaning "Get lost, sucker") but comes over to me after the taping, shakes my sweaty hand and asks me more-than-polite questions about what I've been doing lately. I get a call-back two days later to audition for the director, the producer and the sponsor. Again I do well. They put me on a right-of-first-refusal and I figure I'm in like Flynn.

"Let's celebrate," suggests Nicole over shrimp scampi in our local bistro.

I shake my finger, greasy with barbecue sauce, at her. "That'll put the whammy on it for sure," I say.

"Oh pooh, you're much too pessimistic. And superstitious. Your luck was bound to change."

"I am not superstitious," I say, pouting. "But let's keep our fingers crossed."

She raps the table. "And knock on wood," she drawls.

But the witch-wiggling doesn't work. Mitch phones with the bad news the following day. Get this: they said I was too handsome to play second banana. I was better looking than the lead.

To make matters worse the mailman brings more bad news: notice of my release from a national TV commercial spot that I have been collecting residuals on for two years. Nicole and I try to drown our sorrows by hitting every gin mill in SoHo.

In the wee hours we flop in a besotted heap on the black silk sheets of our brass bed. We don't even have sex. Her breathing is regular. I study her classic profile in the semi-darkness, aware that she is still awake.

"I saw him again," she says.

"Who?"

"You know who. I saw him yesterday on the same corner. He's there every day."

I tug the sheets over my shoulders and turn my back to her. "So what?" I say laconically, reluctant to dwell on the subject.

"Let's do it, Evan."

"It's a crazy idea."

"They said that about the world being round."

"Absolutely crazy."

"Let's do it," she repeats.

I feel my resolve shifting like sand in a windstorm. "Crazy," I mutter again, growing drowsy.

She senses the subtle change in my tone of voice. "You won't regret it, pudding pie. I promise you that."

Sleep comes like a footpad, stealing my resistance.

In the shower I remove the bandage and inspect the cut on my finger. It is healing nicely. I run the hand under the water and the caked blood softens and washes down the drain. The skin is still raw, the miracle of regenerating tissue not fully accomplished. I put my face directly under the cascade of water and then I scrub under my armpits.

I emerge from the shower stall, dripping water on the wood-deck flooring. I get a fresh bandage from the medicine chest and put it on my finger, reflecting that Nicole has a magic touch as a healer as well as a witch.

Her plan, outlined to me last night as we lay on black silk sheets, had the beauty of utter simplicity. We take him to Fire Island and make his death look like an accident I have in the swimming pool where I do laps every day. I grow facial hair and drop out of sight. After the funeral I head for the south of France near Aix-en-Provence where Nicole's grandfather left her a very rustic cottage. Once established in a new identity, I will get counterfeit papers and we will luxuriate, rich and golden for the rest of our lives. I will paint oils, perhaps even become famous at it in my new identity. Chances are nobody will inquire after the fate of the victim, for homeless vagrants disappear into the void every day in the city. In any case he joins the long roster of missing persons, from Judge Crater to Ethan Patz, unconnected to me and Nicole.

I brush my damp hair. Of course I still harbor misgivings. I have always carefully cultivated my feelings of twinship and in a curious way have drawn strength and consolation from the instinctual knowledge that my genetic double walked the earth, a source of potential blood transfusions or kidney transplants, a walking storehouse of spare parts and replacements. I have done a lot of reading in the lore of twinship and my mind is crammed with many esoteric facts concerning it. For example, I know that the only animal other than a human being to produce twins from a single embryo is the ninebanded armadillo. Most small animals produce plural-egg litters and larger animals such as horses and elephants have one offspring at a time. Human beings make both single-egg and plural-egg twins. Our relative the armadillo also makes single-egg quadruplets.

I walk naked from the bathroom to the bedroom that faces west and lies bathed in the afternoon sunlight, my mind still humming with thoughts about twins. Lots of interesting things. Many people don't know that the fingerprints of identicals are practically indistinguishable. If one twin is double-jointed so's the other. If one sucks his or her thumb so will the other. They often have their wisdom teeth extracted at around the same time. Genetic identity. *Sameness.* Both would be color-blind.

It occurs to me that I forgot to brush my teeth and I return to the bathroom. Squeezing toothpaste onto the brush I think about how twins are revered in most societies as a sign of fertility and a blessing of the gods. But this attitude is far from universal. Some ethnic groups, I grimly reflect, slaughter one or both twins at birth. For example, I read about an African tribe that considers the second-born twin the offspring of an incubus who impregnated the mother in her sleep. So they destroy it. And certain Brazilian and American Indian tribes exterminate twins because they regard the bringing forth of a litter a form of bestiality. I examine my bright porcelain caps. Could the killing of my brother be likened to a ritual act? Does this viewpoint make it more palatable? I frown at my image in the glass, trying to focus on the positive side of the plan—the money, keeping Nicole happy, the end of striving, the victim's apparent failure in life anyhow, the freedom to paint. And always Nicole, lovely Nicole. I rinse out my mouth.

I dress in a gray tee shirt and green cord slacks. My tawny buckwheat hair is tousled and wet from the shower. I sit down on the couch to tie my shoes and I glance nervously at the clock on the wall: four-thirty. I should check my answering service for calls, I tell myself with dim hope. Of course that would make little sense under the circumstances. I could not make an audition since I'm waiting for Nicole to return to the loft with my twin brother.

We discussed the plan all morning. She would lure him here under some pretext or other, probably sexual (how could he resist?). She would not tell him about me; I would be a surprise. When we met I would feign great emotion (would I be pretending?) and we would suggest taking him to Fire Island where we could get better acquainted in privacy and solitude and luxury, making up for all those lost years. We would clean him up and treat him royally until the scars of the street healed. Then at some point Nicole would return to the city on a pretext and establish an iron-clad alibi. I would kill him with a blow on the head and dump him in the pool to make it look like a diving accident. I would immediately come back to New York and stay in a hotel under an assumed name. After a couple of days

Nicole would call the local police to say that I was not answering her phone calls and that she was worried sick. The police would pay a visit to the house, discover the body, and Evan Beck would be officially dead. May I rest in peace.

But can I go through with it? I'm not a damn killer, after all! I suddenly recall a rhyme from childhood, "Thinking to get at once all the gold the Goose could give, he killed it and opened it only to find—nothing." I guess that means you cannot profit if you kill for profit. And this goose may be my own flesh and blood. But Nicole's hot breath is in my ear.

Maybe if I devise a method, the same way I prepare for an acting role, I will be able to enter the character's head and perform the foul deed successfully. Maybe if I consider it a dramatic situation, fundamentally unreal, I then can forge the steel to do it. Maybe. I grip the hard wicker armrest of the couch. There can be no "maybe's" about it, with Nicole pitchforking me on.

I put the kettle on and light the burner. A cup of tea might ease my jitters. I pick up a news magazine and return to the couch to continue waiting. I prop a pillow under my head and recline, one foot on the floor, the other resting on the arm of the couch. I thumb listlessly through the magazine, reading sentences twice and sometimes three times before absorbing their meanings. Suddenly it occurs to me out of nowhere that my mother had two breasts to nourish her children; all women are equipped for twins.

The phone rings. It is Nicole, making a prearranged call to prepare me.

"He's there," she says.

"Okay." I half-hoped he wouldn't be.

"You all right?"

"Uh-huh."

"This shouldn't take long."

"I'm sure he'll be putty in your hands. Unless something's drastically wrong with him."

"See you anon."

"Right."

She hangs up. The tea kettle whistles. But I frown and turn off the burner. I need a good stiff drink instead. I take a pinch bottle of scotch and a large glass out of the liquor cabinet. I pour the drink neat. The alcohol burns my throat like a brazier. I feel better. I am on my second shot when I hear the groaning of the freight elevator on its ponderous ascent.

I drain the glass and wait.

CHAPTER 6

I am rooted to the spot, shadowed by a large palm plant and facing the elevator door. Anticipation, thick and palpable, races along my veins.

The mechanism cranks to a stop. I hear the clatter of the inside grating, then the heave of the great door opening. Involuntarily I hold my breath.

Nicole enters first—he trails behind, moving slowly and warily, a tall stooped figure dressed as usual in olive drab, his head craning turtle-like from side to side. The sun is low now and he is hard to see clearly in the lengthening shadows. I suppose I am hard to see too, standing there in the dimming daylight, holding an empty glass and holding my breath, for he gives no indication yet of surprise or alarm but follows her like a faithful dog to the liquor cabinet against the far wall.

"Choose your poison," she says breezily. "Scotch, bourbon, vodka, rye?"

He mumbles something, inaudible to me. As I watch her pour bourbon into a tumbler I begin to feel giddy in his presence and my heart flutters like a sparrow in my chest. A few feet away from me stands a person who, for an instant in eternity before the mysterious division took place, was *me*, and I was he and we were each other. We shared the selfsame entity, identity, whatever you want to call it, the very essence of existence in the very dawn of our prenatal life. It is as impossible to grasp, this mystery of duality, as the Christian concept of the Trinity. However primitive or nonexistent our consciousness then, he was my intimate self and I was his and now he is my brother, my clone, and soon, my victim.

Pearls of sweat bead my brow.

I watch him drink the bourbon down in one gulp. She pours him another. He sips it more slowly now, turns and raises his eyes to mine. He starts in suspicion and shoots a quick glance at Nicole.

"Fuck's going on here?"

The voice is eerily familiar. I have heard my own baritone often enough on tape to recognize the great similarity in timbre and inflection.

"Not to worry, Jason," Nicole says in a soothing voice. "You'll be pleasantly surprised. Come over here, Evan. Come and meet him."

So. His name is Jason. This dirty, stubble-faced man crawling with parasites, covered with blisters and glowering at me with suspicion is called Jason. Jason, my identical twin brother. Jason and Evan. Evan and Jason. Jasevan. Evson.

I approach shyly, hand extended. "Hello, Jason. I'm Evan. Evan Beck."

His mouth falls slack and his blue eyes glaze with wonder. "Holy Toledo," he says, not taking the hand I have stuck out. He seems frozen by the sight of me. "Jesus H. Christ."

"Aren't you even going to shake my hand?"

"You . . . you look just like me."

I nod, surveying him from head to foot. "A cleaned-up version," I remark with a trace of acid. He is a sodden remnant of a man, I reflect. I wonder how, with his build and good looks, he got that way. I also wonder if I really want to know. The fewer details of his life that I know the better for my ultimate peace of mind. The trouble is, I have to at least pretend to be interested in his life to win his confidence, keep up the sham of a genuinely happy reunion. I gaze nervously at the manicured fingers of my hand, still ungrasped, limp as a rag doll's. Then I look up again at this dry molted husk of a man and I have an instant mental picture of myself as some kind of exotic insect who cannibalizes its own carapace in a frenzy of feeding.

I motion toward the couch, saying, "Sit down, won't you?"

Still dazed, he sits, tightly gripping the tumbler of bourbon and keeping his debauched eyes fixed on my face.

"I'm your identical twin brother," I announce. "Did you know you had a twin brother?"

"No." The small word is invested with doubt, suspicion and puzzlement.

"What's your full name, Jason?"

"Plaine. Jason Plaine."

"Plain, as in 'plain and simple?' "

"No. With an 'e' at the end. P-L-A-I-N-E."

Nicole breaks in. "Well, you're not plain, Jason. Under all that crud you're a very handsome man. Just like your brother."

He fixes me with a skeptical gaze. "How could we be brothers? How come I never heard about you?"

"We were split up some time in infancy. I don't know the whole story. Maybe our natural mother died and we were adopted by different families. Or maybe she couldn't handle both of us and gave me up for adoption. It often happens with twins. I've read up on the subject. Lots of people

find it difficult to care for two babies at a time. Were you
ever told you were adopted?"

"No."

"Well, maybe your mother is our real mother. Where do
you hail from?"

"Outside Wilmington."

I feel a thump of excitement at the fitting into place of
another jigsaw piece. "It fits. My adoptive father was a reserve colonel who served a tour of duty at that big military
air transport base in Dover. That's a hop, skip and a jump
from Wilmington."

"Yeah, I know," he says, poker-faced. He seems more relaxed now. His shoulders sag and his elbow rests on the arm
of the couch. He hands Nicole the now empty glass. "Mind
filling this again?"

"By all means." She takes the glass from him.

"Mix me a drink, too, will you Nicole? Make it scotch."

He smirks at me. "If we're identical twins how come
you're not drinking bourbon like me?"

I give him an indulgent smile. "Okay. I'll have bourbon.
I like bourbon too."

Soon all three of us are sitting on the couch, ice chinking
in tumblers. An awkward silence prevails. He sits between
us, gazing furtively around the apartment. "Nice big
place," he says.

"We find it comfortable," Nicole says grandly.

"Is this one of those there lofts?"

"That's right," she replies. "Used to be a small tool and
die factory."

"No kidding?" He shakes his head. "People live in the
strangest places in this town."

"Where do you live?" I ask.

He shrugs. "On the street. In shelters and missions. I
stayed for a while at a crash pad on the lower east side. But

too many guys played grabbie-feelie in the night and I got tired of scarring my knuckles on some dude's teeth."

I sip my drink, hesitating before asking: "Where'd you get those fever sores?"

He winces fleetingly and his obvious embarrassment touches me. Shrugging again he says, "I dunno. The kind of life I lead . . ."

"Contact dermatitis," Nicole says. "They'll clear up in no time." She pats his knee.

He looks at her sharply, then studies the ice cubes in his drink.

"No more bumming around for you, Jason," I say. "You're staying with us from now on. And we're going to take good care of you."

He scratches the straw nest of hair and asks, "Got something to eat?"

Nicole springs to her feet, uncharacteristically demure and housewifely. "Of course. I'll fix something right away."

He openly studies her round snug rear end as she walks to the kitchen. Then he sips the drink, less greedily than before, becoming progressively at ease, more credulous and accepting of his unexpected good fortune.

Soon we are seated around the big oak dining table eating a delicious omelette with ham and chives and french fries and a piquant dark burgundy. I watch him cover the food with gobs of catsup, break bread with his hands and shovel everything into his mouth. He eats ravenously and noisily. Nicole seems a little awestruck by his wolfish table manners, more fascinated than put off, as if she were watching the mating rites of the hairy-nosed wombat or something.

In a few minutes he has a second helping although Nicole and I have barely touched our food. I sample the wine and dab my lips with a napkin. "Delicious, isn't it?" I say. "Nicole can be a good cook when she puts her mind to it."

He gives me a dark look of reproach and says through a mouthful of food, "Everything tastes good when you're as hungry as I am. I've eaten orange rinds from garbage cans." Suddenly he has a contrite expression and he says to Nicole, "I didn't mean to insult your cooking, Miss. Of course it's delicious."

"Think nothing of it, Jason," she says. "I understand."

So, I reflect, the barbarian has a streak of sensitivity.

"Call me Nicole," she urges him.

"Nicole," he says after a short hesitation. "Nicole. Is that French?"

"Yes it is." She pats his wrist.

"Ooh-la-la, right?"

She laughs throatily. "Right."

He tries out the name once again, "Nicole."

As he savors the word I feel an almost mystical symbiosis with him as if I had a direct pipeline to his mind and emotions. He is, I'm aware, smitten by Nicole just as I have been and still am, bewitched by her stylish beauty and sexy ways. I feel him now imagining the fruity perfume of her breath, the coolness of her perfectly orbed breasts, the moist crimson oval of the halved peach between her legs, the strong yet resilient flesh of her buttocks and limbs. Our empathy (is it telepathy?) seems total and immediate and it almost takes my breath away. It is a curious and rare feeling and an oddly frightening one. I don't particularly relish this sense of duality and intimacy with my brother, the stranger. Yet it is curiously solacing at the same time.

Nicole now sits in a wicker chair a little detached from us, observing us with a small ironic smile.

"We have a lot to talk over," I say.

"Yeah. I guess we do."

"But not now, eh? You must be tired. Would you like a bath? We have a very luxurious bathroom."

He wipes his hands on the side of the fatigue jacket. "I must look a sorry sight."

"You sure do."

He rubs his chin. "Could use a shave too."

I get up. "You can use my razor. I'll get you a robe." I go into the bedroom and poke around in closets and drawers. Soon I emerge with clean boxer shorts, a new blue terrycloth robe and Japanese slippers. "You'll find shaving gear and everything else you need in the bathroom." I point the way. He mutters what sounds vaguely like a thank you and shuffles into the bathroom, shutting the door behind him.

I hesitate, then turn to Nicole and ask in a low voice, "What do you think?"

"It's working like a charm. Even better than I expected."

"You really think so?"

"Of course."

I push back a forelock of hair; my hooded eyes convey doubt. "He seems a little suspicious of us, don't you think?"

"He's just overwhelmed. He'll warm up." She lights a cigarette and heaves a sigh. "Wish I had a joint."

I frown. "I'm glad you don't. You're getting this puffiness around your dainty eyes. It mars your otherwise perfect beauty."

Her red-taloned hand waves away my objection and she blows smoke from her nose like the cartoon of an angry bull. "I wish I had a taste of absinthe. Have you ever drunk it?"

"No. What's it like?"

"It's green and bitter and it burns like a fire in your throat and your belly. It's made of wormwood and it's illegal."

"Don't you like any drug that's legal?"

"Sure. Coffee, tea, cigarettes. I'm an equal opportunity abuser. It packs a wallop, absinthe."

"And I hear it rots your insides."

"It sparks wonderful dreams."

"More like hallucinations."

"You're an old fuddy-duddy, Evan."

I stand up and pace the floor. "I've got to admit I'm a little scared, Nicole."

"Leave every little thing to me," she says, crossing her legs regally and puffing on the cigarette with an icy complacence.

I go to the window and survey the dark street. A mangy gray stray cat pokes its battered head into a garbage bag among a pile of trash on the sidewalk. A luxury block, I think with a shiver of sarcasm. I wonder how long the alley cat will survive.

In about forty-five minutes he emerges from the bathroom, scrubbed and rosy, his hair wet, his face glowing, practically a new man. He stands there, shuffling awkwardly in my slippers.

Nicole and I exchange glances in mute appreciation of the transformation. The pauper has become the prince. Not quite but almost. The resemblance, of course, is now closer and more stunning. Keeping her gaze riveted on him Nicole says to me over her shoulder, "Evan, get me the scissors on my dresser. I'm going to give your brother a chic new-wave haircut."

Her wish is my command.

CHAPTER 7

*J*ust after daybreak, we go to the parking lot on Mercer and Spring streets and load everything into the rear of the jeep. Although I notice an odd patch of greenery in the urban desert—a gangly wisteria sprouting miraculously from the lot's sandy ground—the streets of SoHo form a desolate collage. It's so early that no attendant is on duty. I'm relieved. It's better that no one sees us.

We all pile into the front seat. I drive. Nicole sits between us, openly amused and titillated by the situation. "M-m-m-m, book ends," she says with girlish lasciviousness.

I glance uneasily at her and start the motor. I say, "You're going to enjoy Davis Park, Jason. It's really spectacular this time of year and almost completely isolated. The house is very beautiful—secluded, surrounded by pines and sand dunes. We'll have a wonderful time."

He merely grunts.

I turn right on Kenmare Street, heading toward the rickety web of the Williamsburg Bridge. My brother looks very handsome this morning, all shaved, scrubbed and shorn like a sheep being led to slaughter. Even the blisters on his face seem to be fading. He is dressed in my clothes—a striped madras shirt and crisp khaki shorts. His eyes are bright and his manner alert. When we passed Houston Street a few blocks back I noticed how he glanced furtively at the corner where he usually had posted himself to wipe windshields. Since it was early, none of his fellow panhandlers were present and he seemed a little annoyed at the lost opportunity to lord it over them. But I was relieved, even though they probably wouldn't have recognized him.

I drive east and glance upward. The fiery orb of the sun is not yet visible and a crescent moon lingers in the whitewashed morning sky like the last party guest.

He and I had a long talk last night and we learned many curious and interesting things about each other, our likes and dislikes, similarities and differences. It's really amazing how twins, even though separated soon after birth, have such similar tastes and personalities, even similar experiences. That's why they make such apt guinea pigs for scientists studying the comparative effects of heredity and environment. For example, we both are allergic to lobster but mysteriously immune to all other crustaceans, including crabs and shrimp that we can both eat without obvious ill effects.

We both suffer from a mild condition of claustrophobia (the result of having had to share space in the womb?) and we both dislike intensely the taste of chestnuts and lentils. We discovered in a conversation over brandy while Nicole was cutting his hair that we both have tin ears for music (a distinct drawback in my profession since I have to rule out musical comedy roles) and both flunked math in junior high school. As teenagers we both excelled at football and basketball. Jason did not play as good a tennis game as I did but his working class background didn't afford as many opportunities to practice.

Of course we discovered differences too. He is right-handed, I am ambidextrous. He had his appendix out when he was in his early twenties, I still have this useless appurtenance inside me. But we both prefer boxer shorts to jockeys, sherbet to ice cream and playing the ponies to poker. Uncannily we have similar scars just below the left rib cage, from boyhood accidents.

Eventually, of course, we got around to discussing the enigma of our natural parents. Since he had no knowledge of my existence he could throw little light on the subject. He told me that he was raised fatherless by a woman named Violet Plaine who, as far as he knew, was his natural mother. Violet called herself a widow and was very secretive about her late husband. She kept the details of Jason's birth and lineage deliberately obscure. She ran a roadside seafood joint on Route 13 in Smyrna where she half-heartedly fought off the advances of truckers and flyboys and where Jason grew up busing tables, washing dishes and shooting pool.

I wanted to question him further and find out how he wound up on the bum but the conversation was cut short when, after Nicole finished cutting his hair, he polished off the brandy and fell into a deep sleep right there on the couch. We propped a pillow under his head, covered him with a down comforter and withdrew to the bedroom.

"He's like butter in our mouths," she said then, sitting on the edge of the bed in a short nightgown and brushing her chestnut curls.

"Yeah," I said, suppressing a sigh of unease.

"Don't go soft on me," she warned and to emphasize the point reached over with her free hand to cup my scrotum through the shorts. I took in a breath of air and moaned softly, remaining on my feet above her in a master-and-slave stance that reversed our actual psychological poses. I could feel my resistance ebbing away with the centrifugal rush of blood and soon I found my central self surrendering to the bruised oval of her crimson mouth.

The sun now breaches the horizon and blazes into the windshield as I steer the jeep onto a cloverleaf that connects to the expressway.

I glance at Jason and grab a music tape. "Some sounds?" I suggest.

"Why not?" he says.

Nicole, a jaunty gardenia pinned to her hair, rolls a joint and passes it around. I decline because I'm driving. Jason takes a toke.

"Stones, Oscar Peterson or Bobby Short?" I ask.

"Oscar Peterson."

I smile inwardly. My choice as well.

East of Patchogue we take the Smith Point Bridge and drive along the foamy shoreline back toward Watch Hill. Countless whitecaps curl and vanish on the heaving, glistening surface of the sea as the jazz pianist's clinks and silences eddy over us. The day is brilliant and beautiful, a rare pearl of October. On shore the beds of flowers scattered among the scrub pines are dying.

"How long before we arrive at the house?" Jason asks.

"Ten, fifteen minutes," I reply.

"What do we do when we get there?"

"Eat, drink and be naughty," Nicole says in a dreamy slouch.

"We can swim," I say. "The pool is heated. We can shoot pool. I have a billiards table in the basement. We can play basketball in the driveway. We can fish."

Nicole rubs her hands together like a gluttonous bishop at a banquet. "We can do whatever we bloody want to do. Ah, *la vie de luxe!*"

While her tone is mildly ironic I know that she means every word.

The music stops and I roll down the window. Mewling

gulls with stilted gait patrol the graveled shore. We hear the splash of surf, the slap of sail, the belling of a single buoy. I steal a glance at my brother's fine marmoreal profile. Today I have not looked in the mirror as much as usual.

I park in a grove of tall old oaks flanking the house. The motor gives a brief shudder before it stops. I poke Nicole, who has fallen asleep, in the ribs.

"Awake, fair maid," I say.

She stretches and yawns. "Oh goodie, we're here."

"Help me unload," I say to Jason.

Nicole precedes us up the wooden staircase leading to a large wraparound deck. She carries nothing but her head jaunty and high. Jason and I tote two large bags each.

When she reaches the landing Nicole does a little pirouette and faces the immense ocean, her eyes gleaming in the sunlight. "How I love coming here!" she declares superfluously and immediately sinks her anjou pear butt into a mustard-colored canvas deck chair.

Jason's wide eyes wander everywhere. I jerk my head toward the sliding glass doors that lead inside. "Come on," I say. "I'll show you to your room."

With our burdens we slog through the living room, a massive sun-drenched space with vaulted cathedral ceilings and dominated by a large free-standing stone fireplace. I lead him upstairs to the guest bedroom in the west wing. He follows, meek and silent, gaping this way and that. In the hallway he stumbles on the runner carpet but quickly retrieves his footing.

I throw the bags on the pin-striped bed spread. "This is where you camp out," I say, my wording ironically rustic. The room is generously proportioned, with sliding doors to a private deck, picture windows with commanding views of the ocean, a television set and private bar.

He sits on the bed. "Nice digs," he says.

"Make yourself at home."

"Thanks."

I glance out the window. Mounds of cumulus have suddenly mantled the sun. I rub my hands together. "It's getting kind of chilly," I observe. "I'll go downstairs and start a fire. How do you like your marshmallows, rare, medium or well-done?"

He shrugs. "How do you like them?"

"Well-done."

He cracks a small smile. "Does that answer your question?"

"Sure enough."

I start downstairs.

"Evan?" It's the first time he's used my name.

I turn to him questioningly.

He jerks his head toward the luggage on the bed. "What's in the bags?"

I smile pleasantly. "Clothes and stuff. In case you haven't noticed we're about the same size."

He takes off his shirt and I leave the room.

Later he comes downstairs dressed in jeans and a rugged white fisherman's sweater with cable stitching. The fire crackles. A snack of chilled cantaloupe and Frascati sits on the glass coffee table.

From the couch Nicole beams at him as he stands on the lower landing and wordlessly, with an eloquent broad sweep of her hands, invites him to partake of the snack, of unbridled pleasure, of life itself.

Meanwhile she gives me a significant look, a look that conveys in no uncertain terms that she means to make sure that this man dies happy.

CHAPTER 8

*I*n the master bedroom that night Nicole and I gaze into another fireplace, surrendering to the elemental mesmerism of the flames. Lounging, reflective, we say not a word, lulled by the seductive fire and susurrations of the sea. Our thighs touch.

Nicole finally breaks the silence. "Not exactly a chatterbox, is he?"

I change positions, lie on my back. I nod at the pine ceiling. "He *is* sort of quiet."

She hums with appreciation. "The strong silent type. Did you notice his physique?"

I look at her sharply and fib, "Not particularly."

"He's a little more muscular than you are. I'll bet he did something outdoorsy and physical before he went on the skids."

"I've got a good body," I say, pouting.

"And his skin is smoother than yours, more like ivory."

"Comparisons are odious." My eyebrows contract. "But I still say I've got a good body."

"Oh sure, but you have health-club muscles. He has . . . He has lumberjack muscles, ditchdigger muscles."

"Big deal," I say with unmasked jealousy. "Muscles are muscles. Why are his kind better?"

Her eyes glow violet in the firelight as she stares at the cone of the flame. "Why do they call this place Fire Island?" she asks, ignoring my question. "I like to think it's because it was first inhabited by a cult of fire-worshiping Indians."

"I don't think that's it at all," I say. "I read somewhere that the name comes from the fires that were lighted as ship signals here during the War of 1812."

Her cheeks grow ruddy. We hear the breakers crash. "If I were born three thousand years ago I would have been a Zoroastrian priestess, tending the spirit of the flame." Her eyes ravish the fire. "How hypnotizing it is! It's easy to understand how some ancient people regarded fire as the material manifestation of a divine spirit. Maybe they were right."

"Fire is dangerous, destructive."

"Fascinating." She darts her hand over the flames, then reaches over and caresses my right hip.

She says, "Did you know that some people—I think it was either the Phoenicians or the Moabites, if I remember my college ancient religion course accurately—propitiated the fire-god Moloch by sacrificing the firstborn?" Her hand reaches lower.

"Don't look at me," I reply, surrendering to the wizardry of her touch. "I majored in blondes, brunettes and red-heads."

Her hand continues to roam. "Tell me, Evan."

"M-m-m-m."

"Who was born first, you or Jason?"

"I have no idea," I say with mounting disquietude.

The day dawns with a primrose sky and the shrilling of insects. I have slept poorly, plagued by bad dreams and internalized misgivings. Quietly, trying not to disturb Nicole who sleeps like a cherub, I crawl out of bed and tiptoe out on the terrace.

I stand shivering before the panoramic sea, a puny microbic figure on a half-mile wide finger of sand in the vast Atlantic. The moon rides high and translucent in the pastel sky and, before the colossus of nature unbridled, I muster courage from my own insignificance as an agent of death. The lighthouse winks in the west.

It's much too cold so I go back inside.

In the kitchen I wonder whether a murderer can paint a masterpiece or if corruption of the soul forms a barrier to the depiction of beauty. Getting the coffee can down from a cabinet I scoff to myself at the futility of such speculations. The painter paints with the eye and the hand more than the mind and the heart and surely not with a faculty of morality. It may even be an advantage to have committed a heinous deed or two, may lend a quality of black knowledge to the creative act. Through the kitchen window I watch the sun, a scarlet semicircle, finally appear over the plumb line horizon and fling its jewels upon the lightly rippled ocean. Now the wheeling gulls appear to bruise the beauty of a perfect sky.

Bundled in a terry cloth robe and sweat socks I sip coffee at the dining room table. One consolation, I reflect: we will wait a few days before doing it. The time must be ripe, the picture perfect. There is a fine artistry to murder too.

Now the house of pine and glass is flooded with light. I see beyond the sliding glass doors and the deck the tatting of whitecaps, showing that a wind has risen from the northeast. Carrying my coffee mug I go over to the sliding glass doors leading to the deck and open them to let in some fresh air. As I do so a gust of wind roars inside, swirling the hot embers in the fireplace and scattering them over the living room. In an instant the tassels of the Navajo rug catch fire. Rushing to a side table I grab a vase of cut flowers and pour water on the fire, cursing myself for forgetting to put it out last night or at least to place the screen in front of the fireplace.

The fire fizzles out. I inspect the damage. Not too bad. Our carelessness, I reflect, might have cost us a lot more than damage to an Indian rug. This place, like most Fire Island houses, could ignite like the proverbial tinderbox.

I pour another mug of coffee and sweeten it with a spoonful of sugar. I sit in a rattan chair by the front window and wait for Nicole and Jason to awaken. I read a magazine, Town & Country, enjoying the solitude. It is very quiet. Now that the tourists and summer residents have departed, the community around us has a ghostly quality. I reflect that we are almost totally isolated here.

Airy phantoms rise, summer vapor from asphalt. I see my adoptive mother, a small woman, dainty and decorative as a Meissen tea cup—though not nearly as useful—the touch of whose bony hands would always shrink my soul. Suddenly the ghost of my adoptive mother is replaced by another image of a faceless woman of shimmering corpulence and warmth, her breasts rising and falling like the eternally heaving surface of the sea.

I am jarred from the reverie by the rasp of his morning voice: "Where d'you stash the booze?"

He stands at the foot of the stairs, hair tousled, eyes hardly visible above twin pouches of somnolence and debauchery. He wears the same jeans and sweater as yesterday. I am still a little unnerved hearing my own voice.

"Have coffee first," I suggest, raising my own mug in a morning salute.

He frowns. "Where's the booze at?"

I bite my lower lip. "Top kitchen cabinet, left of stove. That's the closest stash. There's another liquor cabinet in the dining room."

He nods and shuffles to the kitchen which opens on to the living room in the east wing of the house, under the landing that connects the upstairs bedrooms. "Thanks," he mutters over his shoulder.

He fetches a bottle of bourbon from the shelf and takes a swig straight from the bottle. Then, holding it by the neck in his right hand, he carries the bottle to the counter where the coffee pot stands. He pours a cup of coffee and laces it with a dollop of bourbon. "Nice setup you got here, bro'," he says after sipping.

"I suppose so."

He nods and drinks. "Very nice."

"Did you sleep well?"

He gives a short laugh, the first expression of humor I have heard emerge from him. "Sure beats a cardboard mattress in a piss-stinky doorway."

"No more of that for you," I promise, aware of the cruel irony.

He grunts and the guttural sound conveys reservation of judgement on this point. "Pretty lady you got too," he says. "Very pretty."

"Thanks."

"She has a sweet ass on her."

Obviously startled by his crude candor I look up at him.

He smiles thinly. "We being twin brothers and all I figured I could speak plainly."

"I guess so."

He walks over to the glass doors and surveys the sky and sea. "What's the weather like?" he asks. "I'd sure like to go for a swim."

I shake my head. "Too cold."

"Down in Wildwood I sometimes took the plunge in October."

I shrug. "Water's a little warmer down there."

"Not that much."

With enthusiasm I suggest, "You can swim in the pool. It's heated and ready to use."

"That sounds like a good idea," he says, sipping the spiked coffee.

"I'll lend you a bathing suit."

He says abstractedly, "Used to be a helluva swimmer in high school. Copped a few trophies."

"Really? Me too."

We stand poised at the edge of the pool, a forty-footer shaded by tall hedges, behind the house. Soon we are diving *doppelgängers*, skimming the water like otters, sleek and swift. We emerge, hair slick, burbling, breathless, spangled with jewels of reflected sunlight. We stand panting under the diving board, puddles forming at our identical feet.

"Got you by about two strokes," I say in an even tone, careful not to sound boastful.

"I'm a little out of shape," he says, also matter-of-factly, not alibiing.

Our heads swivel to the sound of light ironic applause. "Bravo, brothers," she says. Then to Jason, "You don't look out of shape to me."

Nicole stands by the door to our bedroom, dressed in a short lavender night gown that displays her shiny brown thighs and tapering calves. Her hair curls wildly, a medusa's head of chestnut tendrils. The sun is hot now and the morning has the tang of Indian summer.

"Morning, sweetness," I say. "A dip in the pool?"

A look of craft comes into her eyes. She doesn't take long to decide. She reaches over with her right hand to her left shoulder and flips off the spaghetti strap. A brief shimmy and the gown falls to the quarry tiles. Two luminous white triangles and an inverted pyramid of dark hair flash before our eyes. In another instant her nakedness is blurred by the water. The twin pink globes of her rear are sequined with sunlight as she glides, a glossy nereid, from one end of the pool to the other.

I steal a glance at Jason's hooded eyes.

Soon she stands between us shivering in a towel that she has secured by tucking a corner into the valley between her breasts. The bottom edge of the towel barely reaches the juncture of her willowy legs. Using both hands she feels our biceps. "What's for breakfast, boys?"

I sigh inwardly. The moving finger writes, the die is cast, etcetera.

Bundled in sweaters we breakfast on the front deck. While Jason and I nibble toast she wolfs down ham and eggs and drinks a potful of coffee. I muse, is she building up strength for the inevitable encounter? Nicole has always had a taste for what we called, in the sixties, "scenes." I have grinned and borne it for, in the final analysis, it did not seem to drastically undermine our relationship. A disturbing thought occurs to me: do our murderous plans for Jason add erotic spice to the caldron? I've always known that my *inamorata* had a kinky streak but did it extend this far, to murder as an aphrodisiac? I wouldn't be at all surprised.

On reflection I believe that more than anything else it is our twinship that inflames her libido. Thinking of flames sparks a recollection.

"By the way, Nicole," I say. "Let's not forget to screen the fireplace from now on before we go to bed at night. I opened the door this morning and the wind scattered some hot embers around. Burned the Navajo rug."

"Oh hell! Was it badly damaged?"

"Forget the rug," I say. "The house might have burned to a crisp while we slept. You might have been this morning's French toast, *ma petite.*"

"A sobering thought, honey," she replies, picking up a slice of muffin. "Pass the strawberry preserves, please."

Later Nicole drives along the shoreline and over the bridge to the mainland to run errands while I thumb through the trade papers and Jason watches a cowboy movie on television. He drinks quite a lot and murmurs inaudible phrases to himself. Is this queer habit a product of his life as a drifter, I wonder? There is so much about him that I don't know, so much that I will probably never know.

When Nicole returns she corners me in the hallway, out of his earshot. "It came," she whispers.

"What came?"

"The package from my mother. I picked it up at the post office. Barbiturates. The kind I told you about that are hard to trace."

"Oh." I look gloomy.

"Buck up." She gives my crotch a squeeze and walks away, swaying her butt.

Somewhere in the distance a noon horn blares. The three of us lounge silently in the living room. Nicole plays solitaire on the card table. Her finely sculpted face brightens in an impish smile. "So," she says, hissing with serpentine seductiveness, "What's on the agenda today?"

I look at Jason; he looks at Nicole; she looks at both of us.

Then I avert my glance and look toward the beach. The sun has reached the zenith now and the gliding gulls cast matching shadows on the smooth expanse of sand.

CHAPTER 9

*A*wake, I thrust out my right hand and touch flesh, the corded musculature of a man's thigh flung across her flat silken stomach. I remove my hand.

I'm groggy. My head throbs and my saliva tastes sour. My eyes are still partially veiled by sleep. A montage of memories of yesterday flood back. I lie there, alone in wakefulness, breathing shallowly, waiting for sunrise, remembering.

It all happened against my will, I reflect. At first I had wanted no part of it. But then desire was stoked to life in an unexpected and disquieting way. A mosquito whines in my ear but I lie still, thinking.

Nicole, of course, had a great time, excited by the novelty of possessing a matched set of handsome male lovers. She had paved the way by serving hashish and champagne, not that Jason seemed to need any added stimulants or coaxing. We lunched on smoked salmon and an assortment of cheeses. Sybaris revisited.

Before long we were entwined on the rug before a roaring aromatic fire, our senses honed. It was as natural as breathing. We made, the three of us, a piquant and tasty sexual sandwich, a toss of glossy limbs and mossy genitals, and the usual boundaries of gender and kinship soon dissolved. Taboos melted away like tallow. Our bodies formed a con- catenation of flesh, male and female, brother and brother, husband and wife, sister and sinner, prey and predator.

Our bodies looked very much alike except that I was much more tan. I wonder, will the difference be observed when they discover the body? I doubt it. Only Nicole would be qualified to notice. Still we should make sure he gets some sun in the next few days. His fever sores are fading rapidly and each hour we are looking more and more alike.

Lying there in the dawning of the day, my limbs still braided with those of my twin and my wife, I again men- tally rehearse the plan. We keep him out of sight, plying him with booze and drugs and anything else he wants for one or two more days. Then Nicole announces she has to return to the city on some pretext or other. She establishes the alibi. I render him easy to handle with the barbiturates and booze. Then I do away with him, making it look like a pool accident that befell me while I was swimming my reg- ular laps. I fade from sight, assume a disguise and wait a reasonable length of time. Nicole joins me in France as a rich widow. We sail off into the sunset. It's a simple plan that I've gone over again and again in my mind. It's bound to work. The perfect suicide.

It occurred to me: were Nicole and I ourselves flirting with suicide by having sex with a man of the streets when a sexual plague shadowed the world? I stole a moment from yesterday's saturnalia to broach the nasty subject with Ni- cole. She seemed unconcerned. She said she was certain that Evan did not belong to a high-risk group. No track marks, a pronounced aversion to homosexual activity.

"What if you're wrong?" I asked.

"C'est la vie," she said, moistening her lips with her crimson tongue. "We French are fatalistic when it comes to matters of the flesh."

I swallowed hard, but as always I followed her lead.

Daylight seeps in through the slatted blinds and a limb belonging to one of my partners stirs, setting off a chain reaction of slight movements and embryonic stretches. It is as if our nervous systems were fused and I cannot tell what body part belongs to whom and whose brain has sparked the currents that charge us into motion. But now, suddenly, we are all moving, hands exploring, nerve endings tingling, sap running.

Before long, still on my back, I watch through hooded and sated eyes the curl-thatched head of Nicole bobbing like a Muslim at prayer as she alternates her oral ministrations between one and the other of us. At the moment of crisis I clasp my brother's mouse-warm hand and soon our juices mingle in her mouth as in the life we shared before the auroral glimmerings of memory and mind.

"Another picture-perfect day," Nicole observes at breakfast, gazing out of the window at the light blue sky chiffoned with drifting white clouds. She sips tea with a pleased expression.

I see Jason's mouth arch over his coffee mug. "What's there to do around here anyway?" he asks.

"You're not bored, are you?" she says, smirking.

I glance uneasily at Nicole. We have to make sure he stays out of sight. Fortunately there's hardly a soul around outside of an occasional fisherman. Off-season we even have to go across the bay to Shirley on the mainland for groceries and supplies. Our immediate neighbors are all summer residents, long gone.

"I'm sure we'll find something to divert us," Nicole says mockingly, rolling the first joint of the day. She wears a gray sweat shirt and red plaid shorts. Her bare red-taloned feet are propped on the table.

I marvel at her apparent ease of conscience and the way she can enjoy sensual pleasures even while hatching death. I wonder in amazement at her mantis-like ability to devour her mating partner. In an odd way my grasp of her cruel nature increases my admiration and love for her. For I am no better, am I, with all my vaunted squeamishness?

We finish breakfast and before long we are at it again, a trio of writhing and shuddering, a living Laocoon of sex. Nicole wields the baton, mistress of the game. We are merely her matched toys.

Later I drive over the bridge to the mainland to pick up some groceries and things. I drive east under a rosy evening sky and wonder if the game will proceed in my absence. I feel a sudden stab of jealousy as I careen over the dunes. Offshore I see a fishing boat plow a white furrow in the water.

I press down on the gas pedal, asking myself: of whom am I jealous, my brother or my wife? Or both? I have a mental picture of them coupling on the floor before the fire and my cheeks redden with a sharp mercurial emotion as the jeep bounces along.

I reach the shopping mall. I rush through the errands, abandoning my usually meticulous methods of consulting lists, comparing prices and counting change. In this abstracted mood I forget to gas up the jeep and have to double back to the service station, losing precious minutes. I'm soon back on the sliver of sand, the ocean on my left, the ripe-peach sun blazing into my windshield.

As I draw near to the house I see something that gives me a moment's pause. A fisherman, nut-brown and bent with age, is casting in the surf. He waves.

We are not entirely alone, I reflect, troubled.

When, a few moments later, I burst through the door I

find them before the fire all right but engrossed in an innocent game of gin rummy.

"Back so soon?" Nicole remarks with a quick glance over
her shoulder. Her eyes gleam with a competitive light. "Did
you remember to get marshmallows?"

I feel a little deflated and sheepish. "Sure did," I reply,
toting the bundles into the kitchen. I pop open a can of
beer. I sip, glancing out the window at the glowering sky.
"There's a storm brewing," I announce.

"Goodie," says Nicole. "The ocean looks so dramatic in a
storm."

Jason's forehead wrinkles. "We safe here? I mean, it's no
hurricane or anything, is it?"

"The hurricane season's pretty much over," I assure him.

"And the house is well-protected by the dunes," my wife
adds. "We'll be nice and cozy." Puzzling over her hand for
a second she finally discards a jack of diamonds.

He picks it up. "Just the Jim I been waitin' on. Gin." He
lays down a fan of cards.

She sticks out her pink muscular tongue, a cobra's hood.
"How about a drink?" she asks.

"Sure enough."

She fetches a half-empty bottle of champagne from the
fridge and pours three glasses. "It's still fizzy," she remarks
with satisfaction.

He shakes his head slowly. "If you only knew what kind
of belly bilge I'm used to."

She smiles at him widely. "Nothing but ambrosia from
now on, sugar." She hands him the drink and their eyes
lock. I look away at the clouds massing on the opaque horizon.

Later that night Nicole and I get ready for bed. He has
passed out on the couch, sated as a satyr. We have had a

hearty dinner, fine wine, toasted marshmallows and a bout of sex. Time to talk.

"I saw someone in the vicinity today," I say. "An old man surf fishing on the beach fifty yards from our house. He saw me too. He waved."

She shrugs. "So what? As long as he doesn't see you and Jason together."

"I'm worried all the same."

Now we hear a clap of thunder and rain pelting the windows and roof. "You're a worry wart," she says, looking out of the window at the storm. "This one's a whopper, as they say in the vernacular."

"Thank you, Professor Marvel."

She goes to the dressing table, picks up a hair brush and begins to stroke her hair. "Must be the old geezer who lives in the shack over at Ocean Ridge," she muses. "Year-rounder, I believe. A real Robinson Crusoe type."

"Great," I say sardonically.

"Don't worry. He keeps to himself."

"It's my ass if something goes wrong."

"We're in this together, dear heart," she says, brushing vigorously. "But nothing will go wrong."

Rain streams down the picture window and wind makes the glass whine. I shake my head slowly. "I'm not sure I can go through with this. I haven't the stomach for it."

She puts down the brush and stands up, her back still turned to me. I can't see her face and read her expression but her posture and toneless voice tell me that she is trying to keep calm. I study the curves of her body under the peach-colored nightgown. The silence is long and leaden.

She turns to me and says. "I have belly enough for both of us." She pats her boyish tummy for emphasis.

"But I'm the one who has to do it."

"Like I said before, think of it as the greatest theatrical role of your life."

"I'm a lousy actor."

She casts me a withering glance, making me feel like a snail. Why does she have this power over me, this ability to inspire me to any heights or depths to avoid her disfavor?

"What's the alternative?" she asks. "Can you see me living a life of genteel poverty in a rent-controlled flat in Flushing? Or maybe you'd like to see me peddle my ass in midtown hotels to keep us afloat?" She shakes her snaky head with an air of finality. "Make your choice, sweetheart."

I grasp the implication. Either I go along with the scheme or she seeks greener pastures. She's a tough cookie, as implacable as a goddess out of Greek mythology. That's her main appeal, I believe. She's a bonbon bitch—soft on the outside, hard on the inside. And for me the combination is irresistible.

She senses my surrender. Her tone grows conciliatory. "I realize it's tough on you, honey," she says. "You're starting to form an attachment to him, right?"

I chuckle. "Sure. We're attached at the pubic bone."

"Seriously."

I consider this notion and realize she is probably right. I'm not shrinking from the act out of squeamishness alone. "Yeah," I say. "I think I see what you mean." The admission has a mildly liberating effect.

Then a funny flinty look comes into her emerald eyes. "In an odd way," she admits, "I'm growing attached to him too. I almost wish we could find a way to go on together, a household of three."

"I wasn't thinking in those terms," I say, suddenly grim. She seems to be developing a crush on him. A nasty thought insinuates itself into my promiscuous imagination. How bloody attached to him is she growing after all? Are we interchangeable playthings to her? Even worse, does she perhaps prefer him at this point?

Bah. A belch from the green-eyed monster. Pay it no mind.

She's gazing into the distance. She asks, "Have you ever heard of Chang and Eng?"

"Of course. The original Siamese twins, joined at the breastbone."

"They got married, didn't they?"

"Yes. They were celebrities, made a ton of money. I think they put down stakes in North Carolina somewhere and married two healthy American farm girls."

"Sisters?"

"I believe so. Why are you so interested?"

"I don't know. Just curiosity."

I now remember more facts about them. "It's a strange story. Each couple had a bunch of kids. They lived in houses next door to each other and alternated between them. They lived to a fairly ripe old age, as I recall. Reached their sixties. But when one died, the brother died of a heart attack a few hours later."

Nicole says, "You kill one, you kill the other, right?"

"Yeah."

"Remember, Evan."

"What?"

"You're not Siamese."

"Aren't we?" I fall into a brooding silence, listening to the cascading rain and the whining wind. A long time passes before I fall into the well of sleep.

At the first glimmer of consciousness the dream I have been dreaming seeps from memory. I wonder, is it morning or night?

I sit up in bed. Nicole stirs but does not awaken. The illuminated dials of the clock on the night table show 7:00 A.M.

Quietly I get out of bed, put on my robe and walk out of

the bedroom. My racing thoughts, I know, won't permit me to go back to sleep. I go to the rear of the house and slide the glass door open. I have forgotten to cover the pool and the chlorinated water is pocked with raindrops. I gaze at the hypnotic patter of rain.

On an impulse I strip naked and plunge into the pool. I swim back and forth until I am exhausted. Soon I lie panting on the quarry tiles, naked, wet, cold, my spirit in tumult. And suddenly, instinctively, I feel the branding iron of hot eyes upon me. I look up.

He watches me from the balcony outside his bedroom. He stands there, fully clothed, his arms folded, his stare steady and metallic. This silent observation gives me the eerie feeling that I am being scrutinized by a wraith of myself. I give him a feeble salute.

Without making a gesture or saying a word he goes back inside.

CHAPTER 10

The day passes much like the others. Early on Nicole stays apart from us, reading a book, painting her toenails, getting quietly stoned. Jason and I shoot pool in the basement. He beats me consistently at whatever game we play—straight pool, nine-ball, eight-ball, Chicago. Not handily but consistently. He tells me he shot a lot of pool in the Marines when he served in Vietnam. To give him credit he does not gloat over his dominance of me in pool but simply takes it as a matter of course.

I can't help it, I am rankled. I fancied myself a very good player. I never knew I had such a fierce competitive streak.

In late afternoon the rain stops and the sky is bathed in a coppery light. We have cocktails on the deck, a peaceful sundowner. Nobody speaks much.

After dinner we begin again to have sex as a threesome, our customary dessert, it seems. I still kid myself that I am being manipulated by my beautiful puppeteer of a wife. I wonder, are we committing incest, my brother and I? I don't think the same taboo should apply to brothers or sisters as when family members of the opposite sex copulate, simply because the act is not procreative and so can't leave any biological bequest of shame and horror.

At one point in our capering both Jason and I are standing in the bedroom, our phalluses in full bloom, and Nicole in a nymphish mood decides to measure them. She goes to the garage to fetch a tape measure.

Jason and I exchange sheepish glances.

She returns, eyes gleaming, cheeks glowing, and quips, "Now we'll see if you really *are* identical!"

We stand there, oafish, silent, as she applies the tape first to me, then to Jason. At her touch our apparatus stiffen even more (craning toward victory?).

She smiles friskily at us both.

"Well?" I finally ask.

"Guess," she says.

"Oh come on," I say.

Jason is silent, wearing an uninterested Olympian look. It is a scene of some absurdity, any unbiased observer would have to say. She stands between us looking pleased as punch. Our flags still fly at full mast.

Now she grabs both staffs in her greedy fists and announces, "Two pee-pees in a pod."

We laugh in unison.

On reflection I'm surprised she hadn't proposed a pissing contest or something of the sort. But the game seems to have activated her libido, inspiring her to more serious activities.

We are still standing. Her hands guide us until I find myself positioned at her rear while Jason is in front. "Let's make a sandwich," she suggests in a husky voice.

And so the game proceeded. Now bathed in a light sweat in the aftermath, I reflect on how intimate I have become with my *doppelgänger!* Only a thin membrane separated our sex organs as they thrust and palpitated in the body of one woman, my wife. Our wife? Does this condition draw us closer or drive a wedge between us? What does it matter, under the circumstances? To share the same woman in such a deeply physical way is an unaccountably exciting thought, nonetheless, one that gives me secret pleasure and a sense of shame. The question occurs to me: am I using my wife to be intimate with my twin brother? And is he a surrogate for myself? If so I have achieved the very ultimate in narcissism. And the final act of murder will become a glorious onanistic act of self-immolation and release. Viewed from this perspective the situation seems more than possible—it seems inevitable and right.

Jason and Nicole rise from the rumpled bed while I remain lying on my back, eyes half-closed. Through my lashes I see her whisper something in his ear, causing the sketch of a smile to appear on his now ruddy face. I wonder.

After a snack of cheese and paté on crackers we loll around the house playing board games. A fire roars. I am adrift in a neap tide of thought. I know now that I have finally come to terms with the matter, ultimately surrendered to her will (or is it my own will?) and I feel exhilarated, free finally from the fetters of indecision and circular thinking.

Somewhere sirens whine. A fire on Fire Island? I shrug and continue to soap my glistening arms.

I am sitting in the sunken bathtub in the master bathroom, yielding to the soporific effects of warm water and the sunlight streaming through the skylight and the shoji screens. I look around me. It is an epicurean room designed by Nicole in marble and terra cotta with beige fixtures and a floor-to-ceiling window near the tub overlooking a secluded outdoor flower and fern garden. The interior as well teems with potted plants and flowers—petunias, geraniums, ivy, ferns and ficuses.

The sun is high. I have been soaking for an hour now, luxuriating not only in the pleasures of the bath but in relief arising from the conviction that I have erased my misgivings at last. I am now—in a way that I have not fully analysed and absorbed—more than merely reconciled to the plan. I have begun to see it (in an admittedly fuzzy way) as an inevitable dialectical act, as a creative form of destruction ushering in our primal state of fusion, something pure and beautiful and necessary.

Rank rationalizations, a little voice argues. But are they? I gaze out the window and watch a wren hopping around in the garden, pecking at withered flowers. I think about Nicole and the obvious result of becoming very wealthy for life. Another thought pleases me: this conspiracy will shackle us together in manacles of shared evil.

My body is ringed by an armada of tiny soap bubbles. I study my navel, an island rising from the murky water, and the fine musculature of my abdomen. It recalls the tattoo.

Jason has a small tattoo of the number *2* on the left side of his stomach near the line that joins his leg to his pelvis.

Nicole discovered it during lovemaking as her eyes traced the voyage of her circumnavigating tongue. He said he had had the tattoo for as long as he could remember, since infancy. He did not know why he had been branded this way and his questioning of his mother about it always prompted either stony silence or evasions. Naturally a plausible explanation immediately occurred to me: he was marked number *2* to distinguish him from me after birth, which would mean that I was firstborn. I've heard stories about twins being tattooed to avoid mixups of identity after tags accidentally fall off infants' limbs. I'm convinced that this is what happened to us shortly after birth. Then this altered our destinies. Perhaps I am he and he is I, making it an open question as to who is sacrificed to the fire-god Moloch.

I rise from the tub, my body glistening like a rainbow. I

wrap a towel around my middle and pad to the bedroom to dress. Then, under a sudden inspiration, I set up the easel on the deck and spend the afternoon painting a seascape in traditional style.

Nicole and Jason spend this time together in the basement, playing ping-pong and God knows what other games. From time to time I feel a twinge of jealousy. I squint at the horizon embroidered with the black hulls of two distant freighters. A north wind churns up whitecaps. Soon I concentrate only on the work until I am so absorbed that hours are compressed to minutes in elastic time and the afternoon starts fading into dusk.

I look at the surf and I get an urge to go fishing. Why not, for a change of pace? I rummage around in the hall closet and find the fishing rod and equipment. What do I use for bait? Should I dig for worms? Nobody really does that, outside of barefoot boy stories. I get an idea. I remember seeing a package of frozen shrimp in the refrigerator freezer. They'll fit the bill very nicely.

I look out of the picture window. The trees are still, the sky chalked with high clouds. The weather's still pretty good, but I put on warm clothing, just in case—an extra sweater, a windbreaker, hiking boots.

I get a metal bucket from out back and fill it with water. The bucket will hold the catch, probably flounder or fluke. I decide to cast into the surf rather than angle from the dock. It will be more fun. I load up the equipment and leave the house.

A few dead leaves litter the gravel path. Soon my boots are sinking deep into the sand as I cross the dunes toward the ocean. It's warmer than I expected so, when I reach the shoreline, I remove the windbreaker, take off boots and socks, and dig my toes into the wet sand. The surf breaks gently at my feet. I bait the hook with two shrimps. I chuckle at recalling an oxymoron—jumbo shrimp. I plant my feet firmly in the sand, draw back the rod and, flicking my wrists, swing it forward, sending fly, bait and hook far out on the gray surface of the water. I watch the red plastic float bob on the swells. I feel relatively peaceful for the first time in a long while, cradling the butt of the fishing rod against my right hip and communing with the meshed elements of sky and sea.

It takes me two hours to reel in three plump flatfish, now wriggling in their death rattles in the bucket. It will be dark soon, but I cast again into the water. I'm startled by the sound of a voice—more of a croak—behind me.

"Hey, Bub, any luck?"

I turn around with a frown and face an old man, gnarled as a tree trunk and swarthy as a gypsy. He holds a bamboo fishing pole in his leathery hand and a pipe is stuck between his dry lips. Not waiting for a reply to his question the old man observes, "Pretty nice weather for this time of year, ain't it?"

"Yes," I say laconically, shifting my gaze to the float that jumps and dances in the waves. I don't want to encourage a conversation. I probably should never have come out here. I look again at the stranger whose broad-brimmed khaki safari hat is festooned with fishing hooks and lures. My body stiffens.

The old man notices the fish in the bucket. "See yuh caught a few old codgers, eh Son?"

I look at the fish with a quizzical expression. "Old?"

"You bet."

Even though I know I should cut this short, I can't help asking, "How can you tell they're old?"

His eyes twinkle, showing that he's glad I asked. "Well," he says, "they got both eyes on the same side of the body— the upper side." He pokes the fish with the cane he's been leaning on. "You see, when they're young these critters are normal-like, with eyes on both sides of their bodies. But when they start to get on in years their bodies start to flatten out, and one eye moseys over the top of the head to the other side. Then they have to swim blind side up to catch their dinner and they gradually sink to the bottom. It's kind of a nasty trick nature performs on them." He peers at me. "Have I seen you around here before?"

I shrug and watch the bobbing lure.

The old man is undeterred in his role of quidnunc. "Live around here?"

"Not far," I say.

The old man jerks a finger over his shoulder. "Got me a shack down a' ways," he says. "Been living here since before the flood. They all try to get me to sell out—fancypants real estate fellers, the feds who built the ranger station. But I've managed to cling like an old barnacle to what's mine. Only one force is gonna move me off this old reef and I guess you can figure out what that is. I'm part Shinnecock injun, yuh know, and as stubborn as a halfbreed mule."

I grunt impatiently.

He squints at me. I pretend not to notice. He sighs, sinks his cane into the sand and hoists the bamboo pole onto his stooped shoulders. "Don't mean to bother you none. Just passing the time of day."

"Sure enough."

"Guess I'll head over to the pier and do a little angling myself. Seem to be biting pretty good this evening."

I give him a mock salute.

"See yuh 'round," says the old-timer, pointing the tip of his cane to the north.

"Uh-huh."

Sidelong I watch the bent figure vanish into a grove of pine trees. I breast a small wave of panic as I reel in the fishing line. I should have kept out of sight and not made contact with anybody. But, as Nicole said, everything will be fine as long as nobody sees me and Jason together. So what am I worrying about? I pick up my boots and windbreaker, shoulder the fishing rod and gear, and carry the bucket of fish back to the house.

I put the bucket on the deck and sink into a canvas chair. I study my painting for a while. Then I shrug, get up and cover the easel with an oilcloth. As I wash the brushes Nicole comes out on the deck. She carries a mixed drink over ice that tinkles as she sits in a deck chair. "Can I see what you painted?" she asks, sipping from the drink.

I hunch my shoulders and go over and remove the cloth.

"Pretty," she says, after a pause.

I nod. "That's exactly the trouble." I cover the painting again and jerk my head at the bucket. "I caught us dinner."

She glances at the bucket. The fish on top is still flopping its tail. "Oh goodie, fresh fish," she says.

I decide not to tell her about running into the old man. Why worry her unnecessarily? "Where's Jason?" I ask.

"Napping," she says, stirring the drink, a lemony concoction. Then she says, "I almost spilled the beans."

I dart her a quizzical glance. "Come again?"

"I mean, I mistook him for you, dearest. Not surprising when you think about it. Don't worry. I covered my tracks very well. I'm fairly quick on the uptake." She smiles over the cocktail glass in a self-congratulatory way. Then she gazes at the gathering darkness over the beach and observes, "Wind's getting pretty strong. That's good. Drives the mosquitoes away. Notice how late in the season they've been hanging around?"

"What happened exactly? Between you and Jason, I mean?" I sit down to listen.

"I cornered him in the kitchen after breakfast. I whispered to him that I would head back to the city tomorrow and that the coast would be clear. Words to that effect. I didn't say anything very specific or incriminating. He was more puzzled than anything else."

"Well?" I say impatiently. "How did you manage to cover it up?"

"In an instant I knew it wasn't you. Something in his reaction. And he has a brutal kind of honesty in his eyes that you, dear heart, lack utterly. I turned the thing into a joke, said that the coast would be clear for you two to become better acquainted with me out of the way. I'm absolutely positive he bought it. But, I repeat, it was a very close call."

"I'll bet it was." I rise from the chair. "I'm getting myself a drink." When I return I ask her, *"Are* you going into the city tomorrow?"

"I think the time has come, don't you? Why prolong it?"

"You sure you've had quite enough fun?" I ask drily.

"Quite enough," she replies, ignoring my sarcasm. "The fatted calf is ready, wouldn't you say?" She fixes me with a lingering look. "Yet do I fear thy nature," she quotes. "It is too full of the milk of human kindness."

Although I haven't done Shakespeare since college I get the point. But I disagree with it. "Nah, I'm just chicken-hearted." Then I add, my voice firm, "But don't worry."

"I can count on you, can't I?"

"You can count on me."

She gets up from the chair and crosses over to embrace me. She kisses me on the lips, her hands kneading my shoulders and back. "This is to give you courage," she says.

"I don't need any," I say. "That remark about being chicken-hearted was just a joke. I'm resolved. I'm confident too. You really haven't a thing to worry about."

She raises her eyebrows, surprised and pleased. "I'm glad to hear it." She kisses me again, her tongue darting in my mouth like a lizard's.

"You leaving bright and early?" I ask.

She nods. "Will you run me over to Patchogue?"

"Okay. Can we trust him alone?"

"I guess so. I won't be gone that long and so far he's shown no inclination to want to venture out. Everything he desires is right here in the liquor cabinet. Besides he usually sleeps late and we'll get up at the crack of dawn. You might even be back before he gets out of bed." She gives me a wicked smile. "I'll make an extra effort to tire him out tonight. Give him a big send-off."

I frown. I'm sure that the remark was made to needle my jealousy as well as for its practical import.

"You have the plan straight in your mind?" she asks.

"Yes."

Her eyes flash. "Do it quickly. The sooner the better."

"I will," I promise. "I will."

"The barbiturates are in my ditty bag in the cabinet under the sink. Just give him a small dose. He won't taste it in the bourbon."

"Gotcha."

"Good," she says leaning over and giving me a sisterly peck on the cheek.

I suddenly feel somewhat overwhelmed. "Tomorrow. I'll do it tomorrow."

"Yes," she says, now planting a flurry of kisses on my grim face. "Tomorrow, darling. Tomorrow."

She leaves me alone on the deck before a plummeting orange sun. Somewhere in the distance a siren wails again. I feel curiously calm.

CHAPTER 11

The barrier island that we inhabit stands as a sandy shield against the buffeting ocean. At its back the ferry boats carry magical floating pools of electric light over the onyx waters of the Great South Bay. Wild brant soar over the salt marsh, their wings whispering in the stygian night. A deer scrambles under a canopy of cat-brier and dying grapevine. And I, pawn of woman, a potentate of impotence, sit naked in a chair by the flickering fire and watch the slow and stately movements of my brother and my wife engaged in an erotic minuet.

Reflections of a narcissist.

I drink brandy and gaze at my mirror image making love to Nicole for the last time. And for his sake I want it to be good, rapturous even, a white dwarf of pleasure. Their fire-lit bodies slither and heave, rise and fall, join and separate and join again. Mirror, mirror on the wall.

Everything is in readiness, I reflect. Everything. The pump is primed. Earlier this evening I even dug out the baseball bat from among a pile of tennis rackets, skis and scuba diving gear stored in the garage. I left it by the pool.

Nicole, who was on the phone in the bedroom at the time, saw me put it there and nodded approvingly through the glass doors.

I went inside. "Who you talking to?" I asked.

"André," she said, holding her hand over the mouthpiece. "I'm making an appointment for when I get back."

I looked sour. I marveled that she could think of pumping iron at a time like this.

Now I watch the rippling muscles of her boyish abdomen as she straddles his pelvis. He rolls his eyes backward and groans with pleasure. She leans back on the heels of her hands and grinds her pubic bone into his. I feel my own member begin to stiffen as I watch.

Reflections of a narcissist.

His hands caress her hard pear-stem nipples. She reaches back and kneads his scrotum. They jostle and writhe. My penis is now encased in my fist. Onan was a narcissist.

She leans forward and rides him like a horse, slapping his chin with her breasts. With both hands he spreads apart the cheeks of her bottom and arches his back to penetrate her more deeply. The frenum itches pleasurably under my thumb.

The tempo of their movements quickens, and of mine. She draws her knees up to her shoulder blades and imitates a mortar and pestle. He heaves a sigh of high pleasure mingled with the pain of manly restraint. His arms go limp. My hand becomes a blur.

Their throaty cries are heard above the ululations of the wind and the roar of the surf. Breathlessly I pump jets of semen into the ebbing fire.

He sleeps stentoriously in front of the fire.

"Shall we leave him there or bring him to bed?"

"He's peaceful enough," she says. "Let him stay." She

gazes down at his moppet-limber form and shakes her curly head. "I think I'm gonna miss him."

My forefinger flies to my lips. "Hush."

She waves away my concern. "He's dead to the world." Then she notices my pout. She smiles. "The green-eyed monster, eh? That's good. It will give you an extra incentive."

My arms folded across my chest, I look down at him too. "I'm ready."

"Good." Her hand clasps mine. "Let's go to bed."

"To sleep?" I ask.

She yawns against her knuckles and flashes her pearly bridgework. "To sleep," she says.

"I can't believe it," I say, shaking my head in irony. "Venus retires to the scallop shell."

We go to bed. Naturally before long she is sleeping soundly, a marvel of mock innocence. But I lie awake or doze fitfully throughout the dreamless night.

Nicole and I climb into the jeep and leave Fire Island under a canopy of clouds. The morning is muggy and breezy and we're fairly silent on the bumpy trip to Patchogue. The silence that hangs between us is the kind that marks being on the threshold of a momentous event. My nerves tingle with an odd mixture of fear and excitement. The weather this morning is more raw than the kind we've been having lately. As we expel our breath, vapors drift out of our mouths.

We drive through the towns of Shirley and Mastic and pick up the Montauk Highway. I suddenly realize that my silence is methodical, that as an actor I am mentally, physically and emotionally preparing myself for the role I am about to play in real life, the biggest role of my life, a protagonist as foul and fair as any Thane of Cawdor who sets about to kill a kinsman under the goad of a sleepless and ambitious wife.

On the station platform, waiting for the train to pull in, we cling tightly to each other. "Now," she says, brushing a stray lock of sandy hair from my brow, "you're all set, right?"

I nod. "All set."

She peers into my eyes, obviously searching for signs of indecision. "No second thoughts? No scruples? No chickening out?"

I wag my head.

"Think of the gaming tables at Monte Carlo. Think of a red Ferrari. A yacht. Think of the gorgeous light in Provence, perfect for painting . . ."

I frown. "I don't need a pep talk. I'll take care of everything."

She hugs me again, her hands roaming downward and kneading the ovals of my buttocks. I hold her at arms length and ask, "When will we see each other again?"

She bites her lips and shakes her head. "I don't know. It will be risky for a while. Call me tomorrow, duck. Maybe we can meet secretly if we're really careful."

"I'm going to miss you like hell."

She goggles at me. "Um. Me too."

We kiss. I hear the train whistle in the distance. Nicole picks up her canvas bag and we hold hands. Other passengers, mostly men in suits, fold up newspapers and stick them under their arms. A few paces away a young couple melts together in a long lingering kiss.

"I'll call you tonight," I say.

She furrows her brow. "No, I said tomorrow. I plan to be out in public all day and all evening, very visible. I'll go to my weight-lifting class this afternoon, eat out tonight at one of the regular hangouts where I'll be seen by a lot of people. I'll tell everybody you stayed out here to do some painting."

The train pulls into the station and stops with a shrill grinding of brakes. Passengers step aboard.

I'm not satisfied. "I'll call you late at the loft," I insist.

She sighs, giving in. "All right. But keep as low a profile as possible, potato pie. We have to make this thing work."

I nod. Our fingertips separate. We hear the last shouts of the conductors. A whistle toots. She blows me a kiss and boards the train. I wave goodbye to her, a white blur at the window. I stand on the platform for a long time, thinking, feeling very much alone. Then I head back to the jeep.

I walk slowly toward the parking lot where birds chirp in dessicating trees. I think about how much I love Nicole and how much of a curse it is to be hitched up to such a wicked enchantress. But I think I also take perverse pleasure in the idea of bondage to her. It seems to give dramatic form and interest to my life. I pass a ladder mounted by a man painting the clapboard side of the stationmaster's building. I move a few paces away to avoid getting spattered.

Fratricide, it's a funny word, I reflect. Fratricide. I will become a character in a Greek tragedy. I reach the jeep.

I mentally rehearse again as I start the motor, slip it into gear and feed it gas. I will drop a pill in the booze, just one, just enough to slow down his reflexes even more than the alcohol will. Then I'll challenge him to another race in the pool, as many laps as I can talk him into. Then what?

Passing through Bellport I preview the rest of the plan. It will be night, dark and wombing. I won't bother to turn on the pool lights. I assure myself that pool accidents are quite common. I'm always reading about people diving in pools and hitting bottom or hitting the sides, maiming themselves, paralyzing themselves, drowning. It happens all the time, especially out here.

I raise my chin at the ribbon of road ahead. I will set it up with a stopwatch so we can swim one at a time. Then when he surfaces I will bash him on the head with the baseball bat I have planted by the pool. I'll hit him with all my might. He doesn't stand a chance. It will be over in an instant.

What if he doesn't die from the blow? Just for the sake of argument. He would be dazed and enervated by the alcohol and drugs and from the effort of swimming against the clock. I could easily hold him under until he drowns. But it shouldn't be necessary. That gives me an idea: whether he is conscious or unconscious, I should hold him under until his lungs fill with water so the autopsy will look good. I picture it, all the oxygen expelled, replaced by carbonic acid, the blood brackish, gorging the veins, darkening the face, making him look like a true drowning victim who hit his head on the side of the pool.

I pass a billboard advertising suntan lotion featuring a blonde in a yellow bikini. I reflect, heart failure will probably occur too. Drowning is a violent death, accidental or not, and it is hard to tell the difference *ex post facto.* I know this because Nicole, with all her knowledge of medical matters, has briefed me.

Turning south toward Shirley I begin to fret a little. What if, for some reason, Jason does not accept the challenge to a swimming race? Then I'll just bash him over the head and drown him in the pool. He'll be off his guard and I'll have no problem. We're sure to collect on the insurance. Even if the police end up suspecting the killing was caused by a prowler or something and was not accidental, Nicole will have an air-tight alibi. There will be no evidence whatsoever of her having arranged the killing and, certainly, they will not suspect Evan Beck of killing Evan Beck.

I stop for a traffic light. A kid rides a skateboard across my lane. All in all, I think, it will be best if his death appears to be caused by a pool accident. There will be less probing, fewer questions asked.

The sun, still low on the horizon, breaks through a mesh of clouds as I cioss the Smith Point Bridge. Everything looks deserted. I try thinking about other things, to give myself a break from the tension. But I don't succeed in erasing it from my mind. I reach the beach and turn right, driving west along the shoreline. Soon the gravel of the driveway crunches under the tires. I wonder if Jason is up yet. I stop the jeep, turn the ignition off and wait for the motor to give a dying shudder. I glance at my wristwatch: 9:05 A.M. Then I look at the sky. The sun has been shrouded by clouds again and rain threatens. Fog creeps in from the ocean. What if it rains tonight, I wonder? Would that put a crimp in the plans? No, the pool is heated and we can roll out the canopy to shelter it. We've sometimes even used the pool in winter. Let it rain. But it won't rain. I feel it in my bones. I sigh and get out of the jeep.

PART TWO

Esau's Heel

*And after that came his brother out,
and his hand took hold of Esau's heel;*

—*Genesis 25:26*

CHAPTER 12

As I stoop, searching through the garbage can for pizza crust or apple cores or bits of moldy bread, I suddenly grow nauseated and I run into a nearby alley to vomit. Later, standing over the hot soup of my insides, I wonder what brought it on. I know it wasn't the garbage, for crying out loud. I've reached a point in my life and ways where most garbage is appetizing. No, I guess it was the dead pigeon that made me puke my stinking guts out. Yeah, that must've been it.

I stumble out of the alley. I'm surprised, come to think of it, that there's anything left in my stomach to bring up. I ain't eaten much for days. I got this big void in my belly, the part of my anatomy that gets pitchforked by hunger pangs every two or three minutes. So then and there I decide to go to the mission this morning for warm-as-spit coffee, a speckled banana, a sugar doughnut and hopefully not enough sermonizing with breakfast to make me want to upchuck again.

I decide to go to the mission on Lafayette Street though I hate like hell to wait in line with all those nut cases and

homos. I reach into my pocket for the pint bottle and take a
slug of wine. I wipe my mouth with the back of my grimy
hand, squint into the rising sun and shuffle down Broadway
toward the mission, the picture of the dead pigeon with a
purple border on the wing feathers still branded in my
brain.

The sun is bright, the air crisp; apple-eating weather. Boy,
am I hungry. A light plane whines overhead. There's not
much car and truck traffic on the streets and so I guess it's
Saturday. Walking in my raggedy-ass way I pass a lot of
people who look right through me like I'm "The Invisible
Man." Wish I was. I'd goose their women and lift their
wallets.

I reach the mission, a yellow brick building across the
street from an old firehouse. The sight of the long line of
derelicts standing in front of the place and winding around
the corner immediately brings me down. The idea of waiting in the chilly October air with this funky crew is demor-
alizing, not because of the way they stink or anything (I got
used to that long ago), but because I can't stand the verbal
bullshit the mission staff shovel on you.

I stop in my tracks and consider something. Can I afford
breakfast in the Greek coffee shop today? I search my brain,
still fogged up with yesterday's wine. Then I check my
pockets.

I fish out four quarters, three dimes and a nickle. I'll
need all this and more to buy a bottle later. Of course I
might make enough wiping windshields on Houston Street
to cop a quart of Almaden at least. And the buck thirty-five
could get me toast, coffee and one egg on the breakfast
special. Then I remember that the Greek offers the special
only on weekdays. I look again at the bums lined up on the
sidewalk. I turn around and walk away.

I decide to try a little panhandling. In a block or two I
manage to coax fifty cents from a couple of suckers. Then,

easy as pie, I swipe a navel orange from the outdoor fruit stand of one of those Korean markets you see all over the city. The orange is real juicy and sweet and I devour it like an animal, pulp, rind and all. I stop for a second, polish off the pint and hurl the empty bottle in the gutter.

I go into a coffee shop on Broadway and sit on a swivel stool at the counter. The man behind it, a wop dago with fat cheeks and a pencil-thin mustache, looks me over with fish-eyed contempt. I squirm on the red leather stool and put two quarters on the countertop to show that I'm not looking for a handout. I order coffee.

He hesitates, obviously considering throwing me out of the place, but then he thinks better of it and serves me a cup of black coffee with two miniature containers of non-dairy creamer placed on the saucer. I notice the guy has gold bridgework on his front teeth and wears a band-aid on his right forefinger. He goes over to the griddle and turns over a couple of eggs he's frying.

I look down at the coffee. In serving me, the greasebomb spilled some in the saucer so I pick up the cup and carefully pour the liquid from the saucer back into the cup. Then I pour the contents of one of the creamer containers into the coffee and stick the other container into the pocket of my fatigue jacket. I strip open three paper packets of sugar and stir them in too.

I'm sitting in front of a plastic cake tray filled with crullers and danish pastry. I smack my lips over them but the counterman's watching me like a hawk. I finish the coffee and before leaving grab a fistful of salt, pepper and sugar packets for my stash.

Back on the sidewalk I organize my stuff. I put the packets I've just copped in the clear plastic sandwich bag that already contains plastic utensils, wax paper and other packets of condiments and sugar. On the street you have to be prepared for emergencies. I put the bag back in the pocket of the jacket alongside my penknife and other belongings. I button the flap of the pocket and pat it. I stand there, looking around me indecisively. I'm still hungry.

I continue north, having decided to collect soda cans and bottles from trash baskets that I can redeem at stores for five cents each. About thirty would buy me a fried egg and toast with butter. But I need something to carry them in so I fish a used shopping bag from the first wire-mesh basket I see and I begin the collection.

It takes me about an hour to get enough cans. I eat breakfast in a greasy spoon on Delancey Street. When I sit at the counter some smelly old bag moves away from me to another seat. You'd think she was a countess at a fancy bash. Anyhow the food tastes good.

Later I lounge on a "cardboard condo" in an alleyway and bask in the sun, my belly full and my mind pretty much at ease. In the meantime I managed to panhandle a few more quarters and I feel pleased with myself. A thirst for booze starts to tickle my throat but I try to hold off for a while. You got to pace yourself in this life.

I scratch my balls through the frayed jeans. Crotch rot. It's been—what?—two weeks since I visited the public shower on the east side. I hate that place. Too many games of drop the soap, if you catch my drift. I shrug. You get used to such things. Bedbugs and rats. Homos and homicidal maniacs.

How did I sink so low? When and where exactly did the slide begin? I scratch my balls again. It probably started in Miami when Dolores took a powder. Or maybe way before that back in Smyrna when I was high school hunk of the month and thought that nothing could touch me, that I was as powerful as a fucking Greek god. Maybe it started the day I was born.

The day I was born. I read the printing on the cardboard box I'm lying on: "Kleenex brand Huggies. Form-fitting disposable diapers." Violet, sweet Violet was there. Mother Earth, I still see her through a mist. Why does this strange feeling always come over me when I think about where I came from, like some secret I should remember but forgot? I watch a black ant crawl over the toe of my raggedy sneaker and I wonder again about this funny feeling and the way it fills me with a sense of terrible loss.

I look at the sky, at the clouds drifting over rooftops. I wonder when and where did the happiness drain out of me like wine from a cup. Early, real early. I remember being an unhappy squawking brat, an unhappy frowning kid, an unhappy sullen teenager, an unhappy and fucked-up man. But why? Oh, I've had a good time here and there, scissored by a woman's legs or drowning in a glass. I've had a snifter of good feeling from time to time. Or I've managed to forget. But I've never really grabbed hold of life, despite the advantages of good looks and smarts that I was born with. Why not?

Because *Y* is a crooked letter, I mutter to myself as I swat flies away from my face. The truth is I always felt as if a big chunk of me was missing, amputated off me like a part of my body before I could even walk or talk or gripe about it. And that made me sour, carved a hole in my soul, a hole that I fill up with broads and booze and lots of other things —you get the picture. It ain't exactly an original story.

So I kind of strut through life with a grudge in my heart and a chip on my shoulder. I've walked all over the world that way, through 'Nam and the joint and the crackerbox. And look where it's got me. An outdoor living room in an alley in New York City with a garden of blooming rubbers perfumed by piss.

Dammit, though, I still think my ship's coming in someday. I can't shake the gut feeling that magic's going to happen, good fortune will strike like lightning out of the blue.

Why do I feel so optimistic? I shrug and scratch. Beats the hell out of me.

The wind blows sheets of old newspaper across my line of vision. I catch glimpses of bold black headlines telling of another terrorist bombing somewhere in Dagoland. Who cares? The so-called larger world around me doesn't amount to two cents. It's funny how the struggle for survival and the search for the next drink make international catastrophes look like small potatoes. When the dude sleeping next to me at Penn Station steals my pretzel that's headline news, that's the fucking sinking of the Titanic. But everybody's that way, selfish worms in our own green apples, right? Yeah.

Okay, I say to myself, stretching my limbs. I've waited long enough. Time to buy a jar.

I do the shuffle to the package store, a couple of blocks away. Just thinking about copping booze makes me feel better already. I feel a glow in my belly, a sense of security. For one thing it will take my mind off the crotch rot that plagues me. The store is just ahead, its front decorated with colored lights in the daytime.

Soon I come out clutching a brown bag that contains a quart of cheap wine that will taste to me like French bubbly. It cost me every bit of loose change that I'd scraped together except for thirty-six cents.

I go into a park in Chinktown, the comforting bulge at my hip. I sit on the first available bench. Behind an iron fence some slant-eyed brats are playing three-on-three basketball. I take the bottle out of my pocket and slowly screw off the cap. In my mind a cork pops. I don't want to rush this; I want to pace myself, make it last. I could easily guzzle it away at one sitting but I can't afford to do that. I study the bottle label that features a phony picture of a French chateau as if this rot-gut was made at some fancy vineyard in Frogland by connoisseurs with snooty noses and long fingers. I raise the bottle to my lips.

It all happens before I know what hit me or have a chance to get out of the way. They swarm around me, hooting and jabbing at each other, swinging book bags and flailing arms. When the horseplay is over and the bunch of Chink school kids is gone I hear a pigeon croon. I fight back real tears. The wine bottle, smashed to smithereens, lies on the ground, its contents soaking into the earth.

CHAPTER 13

"Get the fuck away from there," the cab driver barks at me.

I back off, resisting the temptation to plant my fist in his potato face. The traffic light on the corner of Houston Street and Broadway turns green and I hustle back to the sidewalk to avoid getting run over. I give the yellow rear of the cab the finger. I just wanted to wipe his grimy windshield and nobody's forcing him to give me a red cent for it. I curse all the saints and devils in heaven, hell, earth, purgatory and limbo. Sobriety puts me in the foulest of moods and the fucking motorists don't help matters.

I plant my ass on a fire hydrant and check my pockets. A buck fifty. One or two more scores and I can cop some booze.

The light turns red again. I dart out into the street, holding the rag like a flag in battle. As I wipe a windshield I study the face of the lady behind the steering wheel. Even in the twilight I can usually tell by their expressions whether they'll fork over or not. Most of them are like the cab driver, they wave you away before you can get a swipe in and make them feel obligated. This woman, a fat-assed housewife slut driving a car with New Jersey plates, is an exception. The expression on her face is kind of hard to read. She's youngish, not bad-looking, nice tits jostling the steering wheel. I feel a pang of you-know-what. It's been a long, long time.

When I hold out my palm she ignores it and drives off. I make a fist and bury it in the crook of my upraised arm. I hope she's watching me in the rear-view mirror. I realize that the dirty gesture means bad public relations for potential customers in the cars coming up but I just can't help myself.

I sit on the curbstone under the street lamp. The sun has gone down and I have not had a taste in six hours. I touch my scabby face. I wonder if I ever again will be able to attract any kind of woman besides the streetwalkers and bag ladies who have lately stooped to relieve me. I used to be a regular swordsman, believe you me. From Baltimore to Seattle to Bangkok females would drool around me like bears in blackstrap. I could pick and choose like a fucking Ay-rab in those days. More often than not I have to make love to my grimy fist, I'm in such a sorry state.

Two feet in shabby brogans appear before my eyes. I look up warily.

"Any luck, cuz?" he asks.

I study him close-up. He's a shifty-looking tar baby whom I've seen on the corner once or twice before. He wears a daisy in the buttonhole of his faded jean jacket.

"Nothing but minnow biting today," I say in a fairly friendly voice. But I keep my face just frosty enough to discourage a long give-and-take.

"Uh-huh," he says.

I now notice that he carries a pail of soapy water and a squeegee, marking him as an entrepreneur, a more serious street hustler and not just a wino working on his next pint.

This brings out a competitive streak in me and some resentment. He senses the ill-feeling—I didn't have to say anything. There's a silent language, a wordless code among
street types. My guard is up and I'm not intimidated. I'm
tough as tree bark, eh? I've been in the jungle for a long
time.

He grunts and drifts away.

I regain my feet and head out again into the street with
my dirty blue polka-dot bandanna and new determination.
It pays off. In the next ten minutes I earn a buck ten, all
told. If I figure right the total jingling in my pockets comes
to more than enough to buy a buzz. So I now think about
calling it a day and ambling over to the package store. But a
vague instinct tells me to stick with the job five minutes or
so more. I have a hunch I might make a big score, at least a
buck. Sometimes you get lucky and a sucker forks over a
fiver, even. Happened to me two weeks ago in this very
location. Maybe it'll happen again and I can buy a pint of
whiskey instead of wine. A lot depends on picking the right
sort of client out of the clutter of different cars and motorists. As a rule drivers of big luxury jobs like Mercedes and
Cadillacs are tightfisted sourpusses whereas drivers of small
sports cars or cars like the VW bug are openhanded big
spenders. There are exceptions, of course.

I scan the motorists' faces behind the windshields. Then
I walk over and begin wiping the glass of a woman's car.
Women are often intimidated and give you something just
to get rid of you without a hassle. Sometimes men have
temper tantrums just because you touched their precious
cars. To survive on the street you have to be an amateur
psychologist, you know? I look at the coins in my palm:
she's given me thirty-five cents.

Heading back to the sidewalk I notice a small commotion
on the street a couple of blocks north, causing a traffic jam.
I smile: traffic jams are good for business. Finally I see

what's causing all the ruckus. Some joker running around buck naked. New York's like that. Never a dull moment.

The thirst for whiskey now hits me, a gut-wrenching thing. I can almost feel the liquor warming my gut, seeping into my bloodstream and coursing through me, making everything misty and pleasant. I promise myself, one more score and I'm off to the package store.

I look over at the entrance to the car wash. The black dude with the squeegee stands with a cluster of buddies telling a story to low laughter. He reminds me of a blood I knew in the joint, a snake charmer with a heart of ice. What was his name? McGuiness, Rufe McGuiness. I remember having to whup his uppity ass to put him back in his place. Had him eating out of my hand after that, yessir. I fumble in my pocket and extract a loose cigarette. I light up.

The north-south light turns red and the last flock of cars in this lawless city runs the light. The next file jam on the brakes and I run out into the street. Thinking fast I pick a likely sucker, a good-looking blond guy in a white convertible, an antique sports job. I don't look at him too closely, just enough to realize that he looks a lot like how I would look if I wasn't so down-and-out. I feel a sudden stab of envy of him and regret for my own bad choices and false starts in life. Of course most of it was not my fault, I think now, pouting and wiping, just a long chain of bad luck and sneaky betrayals. Am I alibiing? Nah, I just haven't had the breaks. My turn will come, I predict, and when it does I'm going to make the most of it, you can bet your sweet ass.

I'm not doing a very good job of wiping this guy's windshield. Thinking too much, not concentrating on the work at hand. I decide that if I scrape together enough dough I will buy a soap bucket and squeegee. The investment's sure to pay off in bigger tips. Got to keep up with the competition. I finish wiping.

I notice that the driver's fishing in his pocket for some change. I avert my eyes from his face; I feel vaguely embarrassed and hostile. I can't look the male customers square in the eye like I can the women, especially successful-looking guys of about my own age. I guess it's obvious why.

I'm looking at the ground when he hands me the bill. Touching paper with my fingers gives me a boost of joy. He drives off and I watch a puff of smoke come out of the exhaust pipe. I look at the denomination of the bill and the sight of the homely mug of Abe Lincoln gives me another shot of adrenalin. With a fiver I can drink whiskey tonight and also stash some bucks away toward a squeegee.

Night falls brackish in the city. I stroll toward the liquor store feeling good. Maybe I've reached a turning point, an upgrade. Stars appear like rhinestones in the dark blue sky.

Turning left on Spring Street I step in dog shit. Another good omen. Maybe I'm just kidding myself but I can't shake the feeling. Just because a guy hands me a finn? It's not the first time, after all. But I had a hunch and it came through. I always thought I had this sixth sense, like telepathy. Like the time in high school when I got a premonition two weeks before it happened, about JFK getting bumped off. And when I foresaw Laura Mason's drowning accident at the clambake. Later on the quacks said I had "delusionary episodes," the fucking fakers. Well, I feel things in my bones, you know? And often my instincts hit the bulls-eye. And I feel something in my bones this minute, something good. I can't identify it yet but it's there sure as that moon upstairs is lurking behind a cloud.

I kiss the five dollar bill and put it in my pocket along with the rest of the money. I look around to make sure no low-life has noticed my bonanza and taken a notion to parting me from it. Satisfied that I am home free I continue in the direction of the package store, whistling a sour tune.

CHAPTER 14

I give a loud satisfied burp. I lie in my cardboard condo outside the courthouse on Lafayette Street and listen to the dry leaves rustling through Collect Pond Park. I nurse a warm comforting pint of rye whiskey.

The temperature has dipped tonight to around forty-five degrees and I huddle under sheets of old newspaper and rags that I have scavenged from garbage cans. The weather is still too mild to resort to going to one of the cruddy and depressing men's shelters with all the homos, dope fiends, pickpockets and back-stabbers. No, I'm spared that for the time being and maybe forever if this feeling of optimism proves out.

I feel the bite of the whiskey on my tongue and review in my mind the missed opportunities of my life. I should have married Amy Clemens, for example. She was very pretty, tolerant of my shortcomings, a hot bitch in the bed and the back seat, what more could a man want? Her father was as rich as Croesus to boot, the richest man in the county, owned a fleet of freighters. Right now I'd be swimming in bourbon instead of swill and I'm sure she would be savvy

enough to look the other way when I had a little extracur-
ricular fling now and then. But no, I was a know-it-all in
those days, too much the bucking bronc to wear the bridle.

I picture Amy's face and figure in my mind. It's a faded
snapshot, fifteen years old and frayed around the edges, just
like she must be now. But I can still see the sprinkle of
freckles over her nose, the red lips, the playful brown eyes.
I can also feel her big flouncy tits in the pouch of my hand
but this is not a good train of thought to follow in my
present condition. It sure ain't. I put the cap back on the
whiskey bottle, saving a swallow for an eye-opener in the
morning.

I curl up and try to sleep but memories of other missed
opportunities keep butting in. I remember Miami when
Chip offered me a land deal at basement rates but I was too
chicken to invest even though I had a small stash at the
time. He hit the jackpot when he sold to those developers
and now he's rolling in dough, guzzling champagne and
puffing on Cuban cigars, with a blonde on each arm and a
house on the inland waterway. I could have been in that
picture instead of freezing my petunias off and living like a
caveman in this scurvy town. I swear, the next time the
ship comes sailing by, I'm going to swim out and climb
aboard. I hunch my shoulders and cover them with a bunch
of smelly rags.

I often have wild dreams when I sleep outdoors, like a
weird stage show. Sometimes I'm riding a giraffe in a thun-
dering herd of animals chased by red Indians. Other times
I'm wearing a bib around my neck and eating an old shoe
garnished with sprigs of parsley. Or I'm taking a dump in
the bathroom of a beautiful palace and who's watching me
but the Pope himself, for crying out loud. Weird dreams.

I waken to the jab of a nightstick on my ass. The cop has
this bored and superior look on his young, sallow face.

"Move it," he says.

I scramble to my feet, patting my pocket to make sure the pint is still there. The surrounding granite buildings look dingy in the gray dawn. Pigeons strut and coo in the adjacent park. I walk a few paces, turn around to see if the cop is out of sight, and then take a slug of fortification. Next I take a pee down a subway grate, the cold morning air nipping my pecker. Zipping up, I turn my thoughts to breakfast.

I'm a block away from the mission where on Sunday, if memory serves me right, they give you eggs, cold cereal, bread, milk and coffee. But they make you pay through the nose by having you sit through a sermon and church service. Still I shrug and head toward the mission, the rising sun at my back.

I'm in a pretty good mood, what with a taste on my hip and the day starting warm and cloudless. I realize that the main reason I've decided to put up with the holy rollers is not so much for the breakfast as for the chance to take a shit indoors. Like the song says, little things mean a lot.

I drink two cups of coffee with breakfast and my plumbing works like a charm.

In the early afternoon, my belly full and my bowels empty, I roam the streets again and, believe you me, I'm not alone. America's cities are full of us. We're what they call in India pariahs. Calcutta on the Hudson. I know how to philosophize too. I finish the pint and toss it in the trash can.

Immediately my thoughts turn to how I can hustle another one. I live from moment to moment, day to day, bottle to bottle, in a circle that goes nowhere. I stop to watch a small white butterfly dancing around a hedge outside an office building and wonder how the creature survives in the city.

I walk to Canal Street. In a sidewalk bin in front of a job lot hardware store I see a red plastic bucket and squeegee.

Quick as a bunny I swipe them and walk nonchalantly away.

I walk jauntily, mentally congratulating myself. Stealing something always makes me a little light-headed, gives me a feeling of accomplishment and pride. I wonder why. I don't wonder long. I'm not the type.

I check my pockets and count my money. Got just about enough to buy some cheap detergent. Then I'll be ready to put out my shingle on Houston Street. What do you know —a little thievery and I'm in business for myself in the great tradition of capitalism. I'm not ignorant about these things. I did a little reading in the slammer—to kill time instead of niggers.

For a couple of days, believe it or not, my efforts pay off pretty handsomely. I clear over twelve bucks in two days. But I'm beginning to get depressed at my success. It's too much like real work, something I haven't done since I got my release papers from the State Institution for Neurasthenic Disorders, in common lingo, the loony bin. Yeah, I've been up the river and down the river both. But that doesn't mean I'm not screwed on tight now.

I walk west, sit down on a rotting pier overlooking the Hudson and count my change. It comes to four dollars and eighty cents. I count it again. By the time I'm through I've counted it about seventeen times. I look around me. Cars zip by on West Street. Nobody's in sight but I have a funny feeling that somebody is following me to get my money. Let them try. Just let them try.

In the early evening I am in the East Village where I have been lucky enough to cop a jay from an old bag lady named Rosie who has been kind enough to give me a hand job from time to time. We have what you might call an on-again-off-again romance, which means she overlooks the scabs crawling over my face and I overlook the bushy mustache she wears. I haven't been able to persuade her to go down on me yet (God knows how she manages to stay squeamish after the mill she's been through) but I feel pretty confident she'll break down soon. Next time I'll give her a Dunkin' Donut (she has a real weakness for those greasy things) and we'll see what develops. Anyway today she gave me this reefer in exchange for a hot dog with onions I bought for her from a sidewalk vendor, and now I'm feeling no pain.

I'm low on cash so I have to head back to the corner. I get my squeegee, bucket and soap from the hiding place under a boulder near the wire fence on the north side of Houston Street where that funny city garden grows in spring and summer. Then I have to walk all the way back to Mercer Street to fill the bucket from a public drinking fountain in a kiddie playground. I take a drink of water for myself. Now I'm ready for business.

Like I said, it's too much like real work.

I glance down at my chalk-white hands. I've always tried to avoid calluses and, except for my time in the Marines and in stir, I have been fairly successful at it.

My hands, white and veined like marble, make me think about Violet. She always had big plans for me, her fair-handed, fair-haired son. Tried like hell to tie me to her greasy-spoon apron strings and make me into some kind of violin-sawing faggot even though she was one cut above a bay rat herself. She tried everything in the book to keep me under her thumb and even some tricks that weren't in any book except the book of Genesis or psychology case studies. Where she learned *linguistics* is another matter—from the breeds she consorted with as a girl on the Chesapeake, I always suspected. But I wriggled out from under, didn't I? If she could only see me now!

On Houston Street I wash windshields for two or three hours until I'm hit by hunger pangs. I walk across the street to the fruit stand.

"Get your grubby mitts off that," the peddler shouts.

My hand rests on the orange. I knife him with my eyes. "I'm gonna pay for it," I say. "How much?"

Above his grimy baseball cap the sky darkens. "Can't you read? A quarter."

"No problem. Gimme half a pound of seedless grapes too," I say in a lordly way.

"Let's see the green first."

I wave a buck at him.

"Fork it over," he says, still suspicious.

I could break the greaseball in two if I took a mind to it, I think to myself. But he has the law on his side so I hand him the dollar and he grumpily throws a few grapes into a bag, shortweighting me, I'm sure. I grab a cigarette butt from the sidewalk, light it without burning the tip of my nose and smoke it down to a centimeter. Then I go back to work.

By this time I have stiff competition—two bloods from uptown who have a snappy patter and quick legs. They pay no attention to me and I try to ignore them too. Traffic's heavy and there's plenty of cars to go around. But I look at them, sideways and cold.

The corner's a good one for heavy traffic in both directions so when the lights switch we just switch our activity to the opposing stream. You can do pretty well if you're energetic but I ain't very ambitious. I dodge a hatchback that ran a red light and almost runs me over. On the sidewalk I shake my fist and mutter curses at the driver's back.

After a while I sit on the curbstone and count my money, sullenly looking over my shoulder from time to time. Earned a buck twenty-five this afternoon. Added to the money I collected this morning it makes four eighty altogether. Not a bad haul. I could quit now but I'm feeling pretty juicy so I decide to hold out a little longer and maybe take the day off tomorrow.

I sniff the air: The scent of rain coming, bad news when you live on the street. I walk over to the pedestrian island in the middle of Houston Street and scan the cars for likely customers. In a few more minutes I earn fifty cents. I'm hungry again. I overcome my hostility and go back to the fruit stand to buy another orange. Peeling the fruit I dodge traffic and go across the street to near where the Amoco gas station stands. I lean against a post of the subway entrance and eat.

I survey the traffic again, swishing the soapy water in the pail with the squeegee. Suddenly the tan and beautiful face of a young woman appears before my eyes. Is she giving me the once-over? I'm a little surprised when she hands me two quarters. I didn't even put the bite on her. Pocketing the money with a cross look on my face I watch her walk away, her legs long and brown and ending in a neat round butt that sways under a short cotton skirt. Naturally I feel a twinge. I used to have chicks like that regularly instead of just hand jobs from bag ladies.

The incident makes me feel kind of funny; I don't know, like there was some kind of deeper meaning to it. A familiar feeling of regret sweeps over me, a sense of having lost an important key somewhere, somehow. At times I feel like an untapped source of power lies inside me, a rock-bottom strength that is waiting to be used but I can't reach it because I've lost the map. Delusions of grandeur, right?

I look at the blackening sky. Then I watch my competitors wipe windshields with speed and efficiency. I shrug, deciding to call it a day so that I can buy a quart before it starts to rain, and surrender to the warm-hearted Madam Booze.

CHAPTER 15

I go on a two-day binge. I don't remember much of what happened to me, just vague things—dozing on the subway, getting booted out of a Times Square karate-chop movie palace, jerking off in a peep-show parlor, taking a dump in a Penn Station public john. In short two days and nights of sight-seeing in one of the world's greatest fleshpots.

Now in the waning sun I sit on the pavement on a side street near Grand Central Station (is it Vanderbilt Avenue?), considering my next moves. All around me the bustling shoes of commuters scuff the ground as they make their way into the vaulted waiting room.

I'm disgustingly sober, my head throbs and I'm flat broke. That's the long and the short of it. I guess I have no alternative but to make the long walk downtown and pick up where I left off, smudging the windshields of pissed-off motorists, so that most of them will give me a quarter just to get rid of me. Slowly I regain my feet

Weaving my way through the midtown crowds, I take about an hour to walk all the way downtown, that's how rotten I feel. It's chilly too as the sun sinks and glows orange in the west. My stooped shadow grows long and thin on the pavement.

When I finally get downtown I retrieve my gear from the hiding place and start to work. For the first half hour I have lousy luck—nothing but cold stares or gripes from the clientele. My heart's not in it either, my mind's way off in outer space. I'm thinking of ways to head south for the coming winter like a bird. Maybe I could clean myself up and hitchhike (nobody'd give me a ride the way I look now). I scratch my beard. It's been a week since I've had a shave. What a downer! I guess I'm going to have to commit myself to a shelter tonight, entitling me to a free pass to the beauty salon, ugh. Do I have to describe it in living color? The lotus gardens of excrement resulting from clogged plumbing caused by using the commodes for even filthier activities than the Standard Company designed them. The bugs who must think the cracked porcelain is a marble gateway to some Shangri-la of Shit. And the human bugs who infest the place. Quick, pass me the Flit!

But a shave's a shave and I'm in the public eye now.

The weather gets a lot colder. I'm sloshing water around in the bucket when the soapy pool reflects her beautiful face. I look up and there she is.

I'm not exactly the poetic type. But lips like flower petals and eyes like green glass, how's that? The lips wear a big friendly smile.

Suddenly I recognize her. It's the same doll who gave me four bits and the hairy eyeball two or three days ago.

"How's business?" she asks in a sugary voice that comes from deep in her vocal chords.

I contort my face a little to make it say two things: I'm open to suggestions but I ain't no mark.

"Slow," I say.

To show she's all heart she clucks her tongue.

Summoning up long-lost swagger I look her up and down. Nice rigging. Streamlined bow, generous stern. Great muscle tone, indicating the potential for gymnastics in the sack. I mentioned already that her eyes were green, green as a cat's.

She does not mince words: "How would you like to come home with me?"

I make my face look blank. Meanwhile my famished rod is stiffening already. "Okay. What's the gimmick?"

"There has to be a gimmick? How little you value yourself."

I shake my head slowly and make slits of my eyes. "I'm a pretty good self-appraiser. But I want to smell the pickle first. Your move."

"I like the way you look."

I rub my chin. "How can you tell under the crud?"

"I can tell." She adds the clincher. "I've got plenty of booze, food, anything you want. Come on. You can handle it."

She doesn't erase my suspicions but she convinces me they don't matter. But I imagine the worst. Let's see, I'll be made the sacrifice of an East Side devil cult. Or she's a white slaver for a Turkish transvestite. It might be fun anyhow. And what if she's on the level? Do I want another boat sailing without me? I've come out of plenty of tight spots, from Riker's Island to Khe Sanh. And I'm just enough of an egomaniac to think I can survive most tight situations.

I decide to string along, my weather eye cocked. I fondle the penknife in my right hand pocket. I've read about these dames and heard about them around the campfire. Rich broad, afflicted by boredom and terminal horniness, seeks offbeat thrill. Picks up wino and fucks him till his ass chaffs. Lives dangerously, has kinky requests that her old man who has a cork up his ass refuses to satisfy. So when

he jets away clipper class she gives it out for free. Classic
storyline. But I better keep my eyes peeled just in case.

"Okay," I say. "It's your party."

"Good boy," she says tossing her head like a pretty filly.
"You won't be sorry."

She pivots on her sandals and crosses the street, shadowed by me. I sniff the air. She seems to be giving off a
musky perfume. The question is, does it come from her
pores or from a bottle? Who cares, really? Smells a damn
sight better than a Bowery shelter. Who knows? Maybe this
is the turning point I've been expecting.

"You got a car?" I ask.

"I live only a couple of blocks away."

"That's convenient."

Over the shoulder she flashes me her ivories.

I waggle my head and mutter inaudibly, "Too good to be
true."

"By the way what's your name?"

"Jason. What's yours?"

"Nicole."

On the pavement in the gathering dusk our wavering
shadows touch and separate.

She looks like the type who would live in a terraced wed-
ding-cake apartment house complete with revolving door
and doorman dressed to the teeth like a South American
dictator. But no. She leads me past loading platforms and
container trucks in front of dirty loft buildings plastered
with artsy-fartsy posters. As we walk by, the laborers drool
over her and one or two of them make smooching sounds
that she takes as a matter of course. She doesn't object, but
she doesn't encourage them either. At the sight of me trailing her they jab each other in the ribs. They can't figure out
where I fit into the picture.

We reach Mercer Street and stop before a low wrought-
iron railing leading to a blue metal door. She stops, takes a

turnkey-size jangle of keys out of her purse and unlocks the big door. The vestibule, newly sheet-rocked and painted a high-gloss white, doesn't match the dinginess outside. This suits her style better. Recessed lighting makes everything look soft and cozy in the entranceway that contains a row of five mailboxes on the left and a freight elevator straight ahead.

I follow her into the elevator. She works the contraption herself and we creak upwards. In the half-light and privacy of the elevator I take a chance and give her plump ass a squeeze. She doesn't bat an eye. Still holding down the lever that makes the elevator rise she looks at me over her shoulder and says, "Naughty, naughty." Then she gives a slight wiggle. Positive reinforcement, if I ever saw it. My cock grows like Pinocchio's nose.

With a groan of the cab we reach the top floor and stop. A lot of clanking and heaving and finally the door opens.

We enter a spacious high-ceilinged apartment with lots of big plants and comfortable furniture. The light is dim and it's hard to focus but the room stretches as far as the eye can see. She leads me across to a liquor cabinet containing a stash of booze worth years of windshield wiping.

"Choose your poison," she says. "Scotch, bourbon, vodka, rye."

I wink at my lucky star, wet my lips and croak, "Bourbon."

She pours and with the trace of a smile on her sweet kisser hands me a full glass straight. Just in time too. I'm tired of sipping and nursing and saving and since she has a horn of plenty I drink it down in one swallow and hold out the glass for another snort. She pours again.

I drink. Now the rosy feeling spreads from my gut to my limbs. I drink slower, savoring the alcohol and the idea of a toss in the sheets with this doll. Then I see him on the other side of the room.

"Fuck's going on here?" I question her gruffly, my body tensing.

Her jade eyes shine with amusement. "Not to worry, Jason," she says. "You'll be pleasantly surprised. Come over here, Evan. Come and meet him."

He moves slowly out of the shadows. My hand caresses the knife in my pocket. I can get the blade out in half a second. One false move, I swear to myself. I can see him more clearly now, a few paces away, offering to shake hands with me.

"Hello, Jason," he says in a fruity voice. "I'm Evan. Evan Beck."

My mouth falls open. My eyes must be playing tricks on me. Fear and suspicion have been replaced by complete amazement. I stand there muttering things and shaking my shaggy head in disbelief, staring dumbly at the hand he offers.

I hear his sugary voice again. "Aren't you even going to shake my hand?"

"You . . . you look just like me."

He nods. "A cleaned-up version," he says, like he wants to keep the record straight. He gives me the once-over, head to foot. The hair on my arms prickles. The hoity-toity expression on his face makes me want to slug him except that it would seem too much like slugging myself—that is, a cleaned-up version of myself. Go fuck yourself, Buddy, I think to myself. I wonder what kind of kinky scene these two are trying to rope me into. My mind clicks over the possible ways I could turn the situation to my profit. I sip his booze and eyeball him. He's very handsome and clean-cut looking, tan like her, in the pink of health and dressed in a gray tee shirt and green slacks, the picture of casual prosperity. I think, there but for the deeds of the Devil go I, or some such rot. Who the hell is this guy who looks exactly like me?

He nods toward the couch. "Sit down, won't you?"

Won't you? I mimic inwardly. The big fruit. I take a load off the floor, but I watch him like a hawk.

"I'm your identical twin brother," he says. "Did you know you had a twin brother?"

"No," I say, narrowing my eyes in suspicion and rolling the whiskey around my tongue.

"What's your full name, Jason?"

I consider inventing a name. But why should I? I say, nearly whispering, "Plaine. Jason Plaine."

He squints a little. "Plain, as in 'plain and simple?' "

"No. With an 'e' at the end. P-L-A-I-N-E."

She sits down in a wicker rocking chair and crosses her stems. She says, "Well, you're not plain, Jason. Under all that crud you're a very handsome man. Just like your brother."

The fear is starting to vanish. I gaze at her nipples, hard acorns under the cotton blouse, and I wonder if sex will be part of the bargain here, whatever the deal is. She still sounds real friendly and, if I don't miss my bet, gives off definite vibrations. I have to hang in now and see what this is all about. The bourbon bites my throat. Nice. Somebody pinch me.

I turn to him and ask, "How could we be brothers? How come I never heard about you?" As I wait for his answer I think about the old feeling that a piece of me was lopped off way back in the mists of time.

"We were split up some time in infancy," he explains, shoving his hands in his pockets and pacing the floor. "I don't know the whole story. Maybe our natural mother died and we were adopted by different families. Or maybe she couldn't handle both of us and gave me up for adoption. It often happens with twins. I've read up on the subject. Lots of people find it difficult to care for two babies at a time. Were you ever told you were adopted?"

"No."

"Well, maybe your mother is our real mother. Where do you hail from?"

"Outside Wilmington." Why am I being so truthful, I ask myself. Because the subject fascinates me too.

He nods his well-groomed head. "It fits. My adoptive father was a reserve colonel who served a tour of duty at that big military air transport base in Dover. That's a hop, skip and a jump from Wilmington."

I mull over the mystery of my own father or, rather, *our* real father, if I buy this joker's bill of goods. He was probably some jack-rabbit fuck-em-and-leave-em flyboy who was never even aware of our existence. I wonder why I never resented him, this faceless fucker, or why I never had a yen to meet him like bastards are supposed to. I guess he must have looked like us because we sure don't favor Violet who's all round and pudding-faced. I study my "twin" suspiciously. Dead ringer or not, he rubs me the wrong way. Acts a little too much like a ladyfinger to suit me. My glass is empty. I hand it to the doll.

"Mind filling this again?"

"By all means," she says, bouncing up from the chair and giving me a sexy smile. My pulse quickens. I could tumble for this chick.

He pipes up, "Mix me a drink, too, will you, Nicole? Make it scotch."

I toss him the crumb of a smile, figuring he'd like to think we're going to become buddy-buddy. "If we're identical twins," I ask, "how come you're not drinking bourbon like me?"

"Okay," he says in a friendly voice. "I'll have bourbon. I like bourbon too."

I wonder if our dad was a hard drinker. I'll bet he was. Now I wonder how come all of a sudden I'm thinking about him so much. I guess it's natural, given the circumstances.

One thing leads to another and soon we're all sitting together on the couch, me in the middle. We drink together and pretty soon I'm feeling no pain. Her thigh rubs against mine. I look around the apartment. "Nice big place," I say just to break the silence. All of a sudden I am worried about social awkwardness. Why?

She makes some off-hand remark.

"Is this one of those there lofts?" I ask.

"That's right," she says. "Used to be a small tool and die factory."

We make more small talk for a while. I tell them bits and pieces about life in the street, splashing on a lot of local color so they would think they were getting their money's worth. All the while I case the joint for something I could cop if and when the bottom falls out.

On a personal note he suddenly asks me, "Where'd you get those fever sores?"

Don't worry, I think to myself, I don't have AIDS or nothing. I shrug my shabby shoulders and say, "I dunno. The kind of life I lead . . ."

"Contact dermatitis," she says, her hand on my knee like a hot poker. "They'll clear up in no time."

I savor the booze and think, who gives a damn? My face ain't my fortune. Then I look at the xerox copy of myself sitting next to me and figure I could look slick like him in no time flat. Better, even. And then I could have this broad and twenty more like her eating out of my hand like in the old days. Wouldn't that be tough?

He says, "No more bumming around for you, Jason."

Thanks, old chap, I say in my mind.

"You're staying with us from now on. And we're going to take good care of you."

Sure, I think, scratching my head. What's the catch? Suddenly hunger clutches my gut. I'm famished. I scratch my hair shyly and ask, "Got something to eat?"

"Of course," she chirps, getting up and bouncing toward the kitchen. "I'll fix something right away."

I check out her rear end, sweet and saucy, a small valentine box turned upside down. Her motor's purring.

Pretty soon I'm sitting down to a big plate of hot food—an omelette of some kind with ham and spices and things in it, french fries, red wine, lots of bread. I make short work of the grub and have a second helping. I don't talk much. I'm too busy licking my chops over the food and drink and, slyly, Nicole. I study her flower petal kisser and the green flames in her eyes. Nicole. She must be of French descent. Ooh-la-la and all that crap. The wine starts to sing in my bloodstream. I'm twanging inside like a tuning fork. If only the asshole who calls himself my clone would take a powder. A sudden suspicion dawns on me. Maybe he can't get it up under normal circumstances. Maybe he likes to watch. I've heard about these dudes. And maybe it would give him an extra kick to watch someone stick it to her who looks exactly like himself. Then he could get some real vicarious jollies.

I bite into a wedge of crusty bread. Why am I so suspicious anyhow? Why can't I accept him as a sincere person who is happy to have discovered his long-lost twin brother? Why? I don't know. Because experience is a harsh teacher and because something about the guy gives me the willies. More than that, he stirs up something deep inside me, some kind of lava in my bowels. I can't shake the feeling that he's—well, my natural enemy.

I look him over. He did me dirt once, I would swear it. Once in the fog before memory. But that's got to be bull. Brother or not I don't even know the guy. I continue to fasten my eyes on him, sipping wine in a sissified way. Then I sop up my plate with a hunk of french bread.

"Delicious, isn't it?" he says, dabbing his lips with his

napkin like some kind or earl or duke. "Nicole can be a good cook when she puts her mind to it."

A talented lady, I think to myself. In more ways than one, I'll bet. I consider: French fillies are born with a flair for cooking and cock-sucking, right? At least that's the reputation. But I talk only of food. "Everything tastes good when you're as hungry as I am. I've eaten orange rinds from garbage cans." Oops. Hope I didn't hurt the doll's feelings. I'd rather butter her up. I show my suave diplomatic side. "I didn't mean to insult your cooking, Miss. Of course it's delicious."

She soothes my fears. "Think nothing of it, Jason. I understand." I swear, the heat in her eyes would melt an iceberg. "Call me Nicole," she adds.

"Nicole," I say with exaggerated slowness, tasting the name on my tongue. "Nicole. Is that French?"

"Yes it is." Her fingers radiate on my wrist.

I say what I was thinking a few moments ago. "Ooh-la-la, right?"

She laughs. "Right."

"Nicole," I say again, taking possession of the name.

CHAPTER 16

They give me clean underwear, a robe and slippers and show me to the bathroom. I shave first and then take a bath. It's been a long time since I've been pampered and I'm not about to put up strong resistance. As I relax in the black vinyl tub I carefully consider the situation. I could have a sweet deal here if I plot my moves right.

I stare ahead, lost in thought. My pecker bobs before me in the gray water, the Loch Ness Monster. I soap the beast slowly, trying to keep it docile, but soon the massage takes effect and the sea serpent spits into the water before burying its head in the depths again.

I stand up, turn on the shower and wash off. Now I stand naked on the bath mat and stare into the mirror. Clean shaven and without the grime I look a little less like the missing link. Gingerly I touch the scabs on my face. I frown and pick up a can of fancy talcum powder and I shake the stuff on my cheeks, under my armpits, in my groin and the cleft of my ass. I explore the medicine cabinet. It contains all sorts of drugs and oils and lotions and creams and balms and salves and tonics, a small fortune in snake oil. I look around some more. There's a very large john with a lounge chair set near a floor-to-ceiling frosted-glass window. I collapse into the chair and turn on a sun lamp positioned just above it. I squeeze my eyes shut and bask in the ultraviolet rays. The "Life of Riley," eh? After about a minute I switch the lamp off. I don't want to overdo it.

The room is humid and bright, filled with potted palms and dripping ferns. Reminds me of a whorehouse in Bangkok where we used to go for R&R. Memories of Vietnam flood back, making my head swim. Vietnam, where I killed while the LSD lady whispered sweet nothings in my ear. We were nothing but a band of hopped-up hashheads in government issue. I wonder if my brother (so-called) had the honor of killing for his country. Ten-to-one he didn't. He has the look of a draft card burner about him. The boarding school type, you know—lemonade on the veranda, wood-paneled libraries. And bleeding-heart ideas covering up the cowardice.

I come out of the bathroom squeaky-clean. They're both standing there in the shade of a large potted ficus, looking at me like I was a bug under a microscope. I fidget and I shuffle in the Jap slippers, putting on the bashful act, giving the suckers what they seem to want.

A gleam lights up the broad's eyes and she says to him, "Evan, get me the scissors on my dresser. I'm going to give your brother a chic new-wave haircut."

Hold on a sec, I say to myself. Whoa. I'm picturing a character in a "B" movie biblical epic, his manhood sheared away by Delilah. But the uneasiness soon vanishes. A stylish trim might be just the ticket.

Soon I'm sitting on a bar stool in the kitchen with a sheet wrapped around me and safety-pinned at my neck. She stands on the elevated platform that serves as a base for the work-island counter, raising her high enough to work comfortably on my head. Her hands are soft, sure, soothing.

Meanwhile she has poured me a snifter of brandy and I'm sitting mellow and pretty.

She starts by cutting the sides and back, expertly scissoring tufts of hair held between her forefinger and middle finger, snipping off split ends.

"Not too short," I caution her.

"Short is 'in'," she says. "Leave it to me."

She gives me little choice in the matter so I settle back and sip brandy.

"So," he says. "Tell me about yourself."

"What's to tell?"

"Anything. I'd be fascinated by anything you had to say about yourself. Do you like green beans?"

I turn to him with a baffled frown. An odd question. "I can take 'em or leave 'em."

"Me too. How about lentils?"

I contort my face. "Can't stand 'em."

"Ditto. And chestnuts?"

"Likewise."

He rubs his hands together, warming to the subject. "Same here. Amazing, isn't it?"

"What's so amazing?" I ask as Nicole puts gentle pressure on the back of my head, lodging my chin against my upper chest, allowing her to trim the back of my head.

"I mean, all those years apart, growing up in vastly different backgrounds, yet we're programmed in identical ways."

"Programmed?"

"The genes, man. We have the same coded messages telling us what to do. It's like we were born with the same microchip in the system and a buzzer goes off when we taste chestnuts or sip mint tea or hit a high note in song. It's really astounding."

I frown. "I don't like the idea. Makes me feel like a robot with no control over myself."

"You allergic to anything?"

"Nah," I say. Then I remember. "On second thought, lobster. Funny thing though, I can eat shrimp and crawfish and crabs and all of that to my heart's content. But lobster makes me break out in hives."

He shakes his head in astonishment. "Me too."

We compare notes like this for a little while longer as Nicole snips away. My head is beginning to feel a lot lighter, the combined effects of the haircut and the brandy. We find we have a lot in common, but not everything, of course. For example I'm right-handed but he's a switch hitter (in more ways than one, I begin to suspect). I have an appendix scar but his body is unmarked except for (and this is really freaky) a scar below the rib cage (a tree-climbing accident) that matches perfectly one that I have. I don't tell him about the tattoo.

He gets real nosy and personal but I suppose I have to string him along if I want to reap some benefits from this situation. He asks me a lot of questions about my upbringing in Smyrna (not a pretty subject for retrospection) and I remember selectively. Truth is, I never knew much about my roots, didn't even know who my old man was, when you come right down to it. Violet portrayed herself as a widow but I always suspected I was a bastard. Now it turns out that maybe I was adopted. I might still be a bastard. It matters very little to me, as I mentioned before, I think. A long time ago I gave up worrying about what cabbage patch I grew from. I mainly worry about where I'm heading.

I tell them a little bit about my service as a gyrene, just fragments. I relate stories about my adventures in 'Nam, mentioning offhand how I offed a few gooks and at this point I swear I can feel sparks coming from her fingers as she caresses my neck. I don't dwell on the details of my discharge, though. Brother or no brother it pays for a man to keep certain facts under wraps. I also don't brag right now about how in boot camp I learned to kill quickly, neatly, instantly, with my bare hands, by applying lethal force to pressure points of the body—knowledge that came in handy in the streets and shelters, jails and booby hatches I have been known to frequent since my discharge. Mum's the word, right? A marine knows how to keep confidential material under his hat. Loose lips sink ships and all that.

She unwraps the towel from my neck.

"There," she says in her husky voice, tilting her ringletted head and admiring her handiwork. "Now you look very Downtown, very SoHo." She gets a hand mirror and holds it up. "Wanna see?"

I barely glance at my reflection; I've never been that interested in the way I look. But I must admit, I look a whole lot more presentable than I did a few hours ago even with the rash on my face. I feel rocked by a sudden wave of fatigue. It's been a long and eventful day.

I take one last look in the mirror and I also see reflected there, over my right shoulder, the face of Evan Beck gazing intently at my reflection and wearing a cold mysterious smile.

CHAPTER 17

*I*t's a bright summery day when we arrive at Fire Island, a beautiful place somewhat different from the Jersey Shore and Delmarva Coast that I am used to. A lot of pines and wooden walkways and sand dunes sparkling with mica in the still bright October sunlight. They invited me here to party and relax and that's more than fine with me. I could do with a bit of high-life degeneracy, all on the cuff.

But I don't want to seem too greedy or impatient. Instinctively I believe that playing a little shy and hard-to-get might pay off in this situation. I want them disarmed, for some reason. I'll figure out why later.

Are my eyes popping out of my head as they show me around the house? It's got everything you could want in a deluxe beachfront place—lots of sliding glass doors, a huge fireplace, wraparound decks and knockout views of the ocean. In the rear of the house, hidden behind clipped shrubbery, is a large heated outdoor swimming pool. All the comforts of home and then some. A sweet setup.

If we did hatch from the same shell, I think with resentment and envy, how come his nest is feathered from peacocks while I am lucky to get straw and chickenshit? Doesn't seem fair, does it? Maybe now it's my turn.

He leads me up a flight of polished wood stairs. I'm gaping so much that I stumble on a rug in the hallway. I cuss a little, picturing myself as I was only yesterday, a bum rooting through trash cans, and I think that I must not stumble or gape, I must make a slick transition into a life of luxury. I continue walking.

We enter a bedroom and he throws two canvas bags on the bed. "This is where you camp out," he says.

I look around. It's a big room with wide views of the ocean and a private deck. The sun has vanished behind a mass of clouds. I sit down on the bed. "Nice digs," I say with deliberate understatement.

"Make yourself at home."

You don't have to say that twice, I think to myself. I'm going to start making up for lost time. "Thanks," I say mildly.

He looks out the window at the suddenly gray horizon and rubs his hands together. "It's getting kind of chilly. I'll go downstairs and start a fire. How do you like your marshmallows, rare, medium or well-done?"

I hunch my shoulders. After a pause I say, "How do you like them?"

"Well-done."

I smile. "Does that answer your question?"

"Sure enough." He swivels on his heel and begins to walk away.

"Evan?"

He turns around.

"What's in the bags?" I ask.

He gives me one of his sissyish smiles. "Clothes and stuff. In case you haven't noticed we're about the same size."

I remove my shirt and he stands there hesitating, his eyes

lingering on my chest. Then he leaves me and goes downstairs.

I poke around. Plenty of closet space, a private bath, wall-
to-wall carpeting. I strip to my shorts and slide open the
doors to the deck overlooking the pool. I step outside. It's a
little chilly but bearable. From this vantage, even though
the house is on the ocean, I can see clear to the bay side of
this finger of land, more like a glorified sand bar. The sun
reappears in a patch of light blue sky and glints off the
slightly choppy waters of the Great South Bay. I stretch and
yawn contentedly. Suddenly I get a funny feeling that I'm
being observed.

Then I see Nicole below. She had been scooping dry
leaves out of the swimming pool with a net attached to a
long aluminum pole. She's giving me the big once-over and
not hiding her interest either. She notices that I have spot-
ted her and still she doesn't turn away, just uncorks a wide
smile. I smile back. Soon she goes back to the chore and I
return to the room. Sparks are flying.

I go into the bathroom and burble my face with water in
the sink. I wince a little at the sores on my face. Am I
imagining things or are they fading? I comb my hair and
douse my jaw and neck with cologne. Refreshing. My mind
works overtime considering ways to make these little luxu-
ries permanent fixtures in my life.

I go back into the bedroom and dump the contents of one
bag on the pin-striped bed spread: shirts, jeans, slacks,
sweaters, boxer shorts, swim trunks—they're all there and
pretty sharp too. Natural fabrics, cool, subtle styles. I put
on a denim shirt, jeans, a bulky white sweater with cable
stitching, sweat socks and deck shoes, real Joe College. I
hear the clatter of a helicopter above and look outside at
the streaky sky. A white and blue huey patrols the shore.
Otherwise there is no sign of human life around here, no

tourists or yachts or many fishing boats. Good. I like it that
way.

I squat to tie the shoes. I wonder if they're cops in the
whirlybird and, if so, what kind of cops—feds, local, state? I
don't like cops or screws of any kind. The very thought of
them makes the hair on the back of my hands and neck
prickle.

I go down the stairs. I hear flames snap and sizzle in the
fireplace. From the landing I see them seated at a coffee
table set for a snack. Melon slices and white wine. I put on
my shy face and come down the rest of the way.

Later, tossing and turning on the cool cotton sheets, I
think about him. I said it before and I'll say it again, something about him gets my goat, some old grudge I must have,
something faded by time but still there. I can taste the
grudge, like crow feathers in my mouth.

I stretch out on the clean white sheets in this beautiful
room in this snazzy house, surprised by how strong my
emotions are, coming from such hazy beginnings. I hear the
rush and roll of the surf outside. The shades are drawn
tight but I know it's morning. I can sense it.

I prop myself up on my right elbow. I hear a stirring
downstairs. Somebody is moving around. My old rival, I
suspect, the person who I've struggled against, I suppose,
since even before either of us set eyes on the sun, moon and
sky. Or maybe it's her. Alone. Waiting. Only one way to
find out.

I throw back the sheets and stand up. I'm rocky on my
feet and my head begins to pound. Drank too much last
night. I could use a little hair of the dog. A funny thought
occurs to me: maybe I should turn over a new leaf and quit
drinking so much. Now where did that crazy idea come
from? Should I climb on the wagon just when my cup run-
neth over? Not on your life.

I draw up the blinds and light floods the room. Woozy, I blink once or twice. My morning erection stands at half-mast. I stumble into the toilet and pee.

Hair of the dog, remember? I throw on some clothes and head downstairs. From the top landing I see him sitting by the front window reading a magazine, all cozy like. Quiet as a mouse I pad down the stairs.

"Where d'you stash the booze?" I ask. Did I sound too short? Is my true self showing? I study his expression. He doesn't seem very put-out by my tone of voice or by my manner. He raises his coffee mug and says, "Have coffee first."

"Where's the booze at?" I repeat.

He gives me a smile that might be saying he likes to be pushed around. I notice that she sometimes treats him that way too, like a footman or something.

"Top kitchen cabinet, left of stove," he says. "That's the closest stash. There's another liquor cabinet in the dining room."

"Thanks." I go to the kitchen and haul out a quart of bourbon. I take a slug straight from the bottle and then I spike the coffee with it. "Nice setup you got here, bro'," I say.

"I suppose so," he says, burying his nose in the magazine. His voice is reedy, like a radio announcer's. He mentioned to me that he was an actor so I guess he's had voice training. I'm sure I could sound just like him with a little practice. I sip the coffee and bourbon and continue approvingly, "Very nice."

"Did you sleep well?" he asks in his annoyingly polite way.

Like a top, fop, is what I feel like saying, but I don't. I laugh and say, "Sure beats a cardboard mattress in a piss-stinky doorway."

"No more of that for you," he says.

You bet your sweet ass, I think. By hook or crook I'm not going back to being a guttersnipe. And I'm not playing second fiddle to this faggot either. Funny, even though he looks like me and I'm now inclined to accept the idea that he's my twin brother, I feel no kinship with him and no special bond except maybe this misty memory of bad blood. I want to put a few of my cards on the table to test his reaction. I say, "Pretty lady you got too. Very pretty."

He looks up from the magazine with a slightly buffaloed expression. "Thanks," he says in a flat voice. Did I touch a sore spot?

"She has a sweet ass on her," I say boldly.

He blinks a couple of times.

Who knows? I figure. He might be one of those guys who gets off on sharing his lady. I've heard about the type. If he isn't I'll just have to figure out a way to steal her from him. Shouldn't be too hard. I smile. "We being twin brothers and all I figured I could speak plainly."

"I guess so." His face clouds up a little. He doesn't seem all that convinced so maybe I had him pegged wrong. I might have to take a new tack.

I walk over to the glass doors overlooking the deck and the ocean. A sailboat skims the surface. "What's the weather like?" I ask. "I'd sure like to go for a swim."

He shakes his head. "Too cold."

"Down in Wildwood I sometimes took the plunge in October.

"Water's a little warmer down there," he says.

"Not that much."

"You can swim in the pool," he suggests. "It's heated and ready to use."

"That sounds like a good idea." My neck flushes pleasantly from the alcohol and coffee.

"I'll lend you a bathing suit."

I gaze into the distance, remembering my high school

swimming career. "Used to be a helluva swimmer in high school," I boast. "Copped a few trophies."

"Really. Me too."

That sounds something like a challenge, I think. He's smiling in an arrogant way. My competitive streak is aroused.

Jack Robinson and we're at the edge of the pool. I bend my knees slightly and do some stretching exercises to limber up. It's been a long time. I've been abusing my body lately but I still can whup this cream puff with one hand tied behind my back. Suddenly I get this feeling of what they call *déja vu,* you know? Like I've been through all this before in another lifetime.

"At the count of three," he says.

We count together.

We hit the water.

It's over quickly. I lost. I conceal my anger.

"Got you by about two strokes," he says between pants of breath. He doesn't gloat, just says it matter-of-factly.

"I'm a little out of shape," I observe.

So the powder puff can swim.

We hear mocking applause. Nicole stands in the bright sunlight on the tiles at the edge of the pool. She's dressed in a short pale purple nightie and her hair is tousled. She looks like a wilted flower that needs only a splash of water to perk up.

"Bravo, brothers," she says. She looks square at me. "You don't look out of shape to me."

She's bold as brass. Spirited. Outspoken. Hot to trot.

He invites her to swim. She right away takes him up on it, wiggling out of her nightgown and into her birthday suit. She's giving me a sneak preview. Are those nipples or maraschino cherries? Is that a bush or a bird's nest? Yummy. A second later her tail's waving in the green water.

She's wrapped in a towel now, standing between us and feeling up our arm muscles. "What's for breakfast, boys?"

Blood sausages, says my nasty mind. But I keep my trap shut.

The morning sparkles. Dressed in sweaters we eat breakfast on the deck. She has a hearty appetite for such a little thing, gobbling down eggs, ham and coffee. He says something to her about not forgetting to screen off the fireplace but I don't pay much attention to it. I'm still thinking about her naked body. Ripe fruit. I've seen a lot of unclothed ladies in my time but she is prime-grade meat.

She reads a newspaper. I twiddle my thumbs and drink coffee. She spreads preserves on a slice of muffin and looks like the cat that swallowed the canary.

I can just sense that the fun is going to start any minute now. But she disappoints me by taking the jeep to the mainland to run an errand or two. So I'm left alone with him and all this booze. I break down and start doing some serious drinking, choosing Irish whiskey this time for a change of pace. A kid alone in a candy store. I switch on the TV and watch a shoot-em-up to try to get my mind off my hormones. As I watch the movie and sip the Irish I also echo the actors' dialogue under my breath. This is a habit of mine; I don't know where I picked it up.

Pretty soon she's back and my gonads get recharged. We sit around the living room and nobody says much until she breaks the ice: "So. What's on the agenda today?"

She flashes a wicked smile.

CHAPTER 18

I love the way she moves, snaky, sexy. She makes me want to reach out and trace my hand along her curves. It's obvious that she's setting the stage for something, the way she's slithering around between the two of us. She passes a hash pipe that I puff over my tumbler of Irish. The rest of the morning and the early afternoon pass in a fog.

We have smoked salmon and bubbly for lunch. High living. So far every hunger I have is getting satisfied except one. But it's easy to be patient when you're floating on a magic carpet.

I gobble up all the goodies in sight while she prances around, laughing and twitching her butt and rolling her eyes at both of us. He just sits there in a funk and I can't figure out what's going on in his head. Maybe he's jealous, maybe he's turned on. Hard to tell. In any case I don't care a hill of beans. I'm focusing on the doll baby. We sample a board of different cheeses.

I know one thing: I'm ready for action. My head's spinning like a top and my nerve endings are all juiced up. She keeps peeling off clothes as the day wears on. She's down now to a little tank top and silk jogging shorts that show everything Nature gave her. There's a blaze going now in the fireplace to match the one in my groin.

Pretty soon she's talking less and less. Now silence. No words are necessary. She stretches out like a kitten in front of the fire and reaches out her arms to us both.

We reach her at the same time. He crushes his mouth to hers. I'm nibbling and tonguing her naked feet. She writhes and trembles under our twin tasters. We meet at her center and he stops and gives me a lingering look that's hard for me to read. I get a queasy feeling. But I shrug it off and give over my attention to the juicy morsel between her legs.

"Ummm," she says in a husky voice. "Always wanted a bilingual lover."

Soon all three of us are bare-assed and bouncing around in kinky combinations of foreplay—and backplay. At first I wince or move away whenever my brother's body presses too close to my own or whenever our hands and lips brush private parts. But soon I forget about all this squeamishness and get into the spirit of the thing. Let's keep the record straight—I don't surrender to these incidental contacts with the same wild abandon as he seems to, but I tolerate them in the heat of horniness. Now as I nibble the nub of her sex I think about how sex between twin brothers would be homosexual incest carried to the highest power.

I surface to catch my breath. She grabs her own feet and spreads her legs wide. I dab the head of my cock with spit and bury my tool deep inside her. Her arms and legs wrap around me like a man-eating plant. I grind slowly against her. She's very strong, this sweet bitch, and matches me, movement for movement.

Where is he? Soon I feel the flick-flick-flicker of a tongue at my scrotum. Couldn't be hers unless she was some kind of gila monster so it has to be his tongue. So that's his thing, eh? Well, let him have his jollies as long as he doesn't expect me to give back in kind. Twins or no twins there's a big difference between us: he seems to operate on two currents while I operate on one. My thrusts are getting faster and longer. She chants some gibberish. His tongue burns my balls, fueling the fire. Her hands cup my buttocks and press me closer. I'm getting frantic telegraph messages from my testicles. I give another big lunge and her body shimmers under me. Once more. She shudders and salivates and jabbers like an animal. Finally, collapsing on her breastbone, I flood her womb with juice that I've been saving up for a long, long time.

Later we have a big dinner to refuel, I guess, for the night ahead. Onion soup, crab salad, cold Long Island duckling, french bread, the works. And more champagne to slosh it down with. I eat like a champ. Nicole, dressed now in some kind of geisha-girl kimono, stows it away pretty good too. She eats like she screws—with relish, mustard and no self-consciousness. She keeps stealing glances at me too, like I was her main man now instead of her husband. Maybe it's the novelty of it all or maybe I'm imagining things or maybe it's for real and she's turning sweet on me. Why not? Stranger things have happened in the history of mankind.

After dinner we stack everything in the dishwasher and mosey over to the master bedroom that has a flashy, up-to-the-minute compact disc sound system. She plays vintage Rolling Stones and passes around another pipe. She's ready for another go-round and I'm not in the mood to argue.

We form another triangle. Every which way. One time I plug her from the rear as she lies on top of him, her vagina stuffed by both our penises which rub up against each other.

I feel a little miffed. I wish he would take a powder so I could enjoy this juicy piece all by myself for a while without him horning in. Now that's a funny idea, isn't it? Where do I get off? After all, she belongs to him, at least on paper. Then I wonder for the first time: why couldn't I step into his place?

Presto, chango. Easy as pie.

I heft the plump globes of her ass.

Why not? We're spitting images of each other. And I think she's sending definite signals that she might consider such an arrangement not such a bad idea either. Let's face it —wouldn't almost any chick prefer me to that wimp? This may be when I finally get all that's coming to me. Scraps of words from bible class come back to me: "The dew of heaven and the fatness of the earth and plenty of corn and wine." Words to that effect. It would be like collecting an inheritance that somebody gypped me out of a long time ago.

With my rod sunk inside her and causing friction with his, I start to fantasize about filling his shoes in life, having his apartment, this summer house, his cars, his clothes, maybe even his career. And, best of all, I'd have sole possession of his woman who now bucks and bounces between us both. It all seems to jell in my mind as an event that has been waiting to happen. A crazy idea, huh? Or is it?

We now shudder and groan and climax together, mixing sap.

More days of wine and roses pass. My prick's sore and, I guess, so's his. But she never seems to tire. I suppose it's the novelty of screwing twins. Don't get me wrong, I ain't burned out yet or anything of that sort. I'm just a little baffled at how isolated we are here. They don't even get phone calls. I suppose they deliberately didn't tell anyone they were leaving town so they could really get away from it all. Evan told me he was an actor. I guess that means he doesn't have to work but a couple of months out of the year and the rest of the time he can just goof off. Nice racket.

An actor. I wonder if I could have been an actor. Hey, why not? I have the looks for it, or at least I *had* the looks.

And what's it take to be an actor, especially on film or video? You memorize a couple of lines at a time. If you don't get it right the first time the director says cut and you shoot the whole shebang all over again. You go over budget and the producers take it off their income tax. Sure, I could have been an actor. Hey, maybe I can still become one. There's a thought.

I pose before the mirror in my room upstairs. "To be or not to be, that is the question." Then I laugh at my reflection. I study my face, widening my sleepy eyes. The blisters are fading fast, I notice. Getting laid regular seems to be just what the doctor ordered, I say to myself with a smirk at the glass. My face grows serious, reflective. Could I pull it off? Go slow, that's my advice to me. Go slow. I go downstairs for breakfast.

That evening he has to drive over to the mainland for supplies and stuff, leaving the two of us alone. I get pretty hepped up. I'm curious about what she's like when he's not around. I'd also like to sound her out about certain things, certain feelings. I'm pretty sure she's not very hung up on her old man, like she's waiting for something better to come along. But I don't want to say that in so many words, don't want to stick my foot in my mouth. In any case I'm not really that handy with words, never have been. Can't even say it aloud to myself, what I'm thinking. I've done a lot of nasty things in my life, I confess. I've been a bad bad boy. Committed some down and dirty acts. But the one I'm contemplating now beats the band.

I've killed.

I've killed plenty of times and not only in 'Nam. Had to, just to survive. Self-defense, you know what I mean? In the joint, in the hospital, in the street, violence is a way of life. If you pass through the blast furnace you come out with a cast-iron constitution. Another thing—they'll get you if you don't get them first. So be there first, that's my philoso-

phy. But my own twin brother, that's something else, even
if he is an AC-DC wimp. I have to think about this real
hard.

"Let's play a game," she suggests after he's gone, breaking
my train of thought. We're sitting across from each other in
the living room. She was reading a book while I was just
vegetating and drinking beer.

"What do you want to play?" I drawl. "Spin the bottle?"

"Later, you horny toad. I was thinking of a card game."

I shrug. "Okay." I think, it will give us a chance to chat.

"Shall we play for stakes?"

"What, like strip poker?"

"There you go again—a one-track mind." She smiles and
saliva glistens in a web between her two front teeth. "What
makes you think I'd cheat on my hubby anyway?"

I snort and say the obvious: "What do you call what
we've been doing for the last few days? Having tea parties?"

She picks up a deck of Tally-Ho playing cards with a blue
geometric pattern on the backs and begins to handle and
shuffle them with all the skill of a fucking riverboat gam-
bler. "Ah, but we've always been a threesome," she points
out. "He's always been present and given his tacit consent
and compliance. So, in a sense, I haven't been unfaithful to
him, have I? Now it's different. Now we're all alone."

I sit in silent wonder. That makes a difference, I ask myself in disbelief? She's let me plug every hole in her body
except maybe her ears but she doesn't call that being unfaithful? I consider the idea carefully and come to the conclusion that maybe she has a point.

She cuts the deck skillfully with one hand. She pouts
and adds, "Besides, I'm sort of sore." She gently touches
her groin. "Down here."

I grunt. "Can't say I'm surprised," I remark. I lace my
fingers together and put my elbows on the table. "How
about gin rummy? I played a lot in the service."

Her green eyes widen. "In the Army, right? Isn't that what you said?"

I correct her. "The Marines," I say, trying not to sound cocky. What are we, anyway, kids sucking ice cream sodas?

"Oooh." Her interest is obvious. She wets her lips until they glisten and she asks, "And you served in Vietnam?"

"Yeah. Spent eight months in that cesspool."

Her cheeks grow pink. "In combat?" she asks.

I touched on the subject before, but I guess she wants the gory details. "I wasn't playing tiddlywinks," I say with swagger. "Ever hear of Da Nang, Khe Sanh?"

"Vaguely."

"Well, if you ever get an invitation to vacation in either of those garden spots, turn it down. Unless you like dusty sweltering summers—monsoons, typhoons, muck everywhere."

"Not exactly a tropical paradise, eh?"

"You can say that again."

Something flashed in her eyes. "And you've killed people?"

"Gooks ain't people. But I've killed people, yes." Maybe I'd do better to shut my big yap. Then again she doesn't seem disapproving or shocked by the news. Just excited, almost exhilarated. Is she thinking what I'm thinking?

"How?" she asks, wiggling her butt in the seat and leaning closer.

"How what?"

She squirms again. "How did you kill them?"

"Picked 'em off with my M-16, mostly."

"Ever kill anybody with your bare hands?" Her voice grew huskier when she asked the question.

I dart a look at her and note her glistening eyes and moist lips. Then I drop my glance. "Once."

She hesitates. She asks, "What's it feel like?"

I hunch my shoulders. "I'm not good with words."

"Yes you are."

"You don't want to know, anyway."

"Yes I do," she insists.

I mull the question over for a minute. I lean back in the chair and scratch my head. "Makes you feel like your hands have magical powers. Makes you feel like some kind of storybook character, a god or a hero. You can drain the very life out of a living thing, a warm being with blood flowing through his veins and a heart pounding, and make him into a cold mass of nothing, a rag doll with cotton inside. Makes you feel powerful, you know what I mean? Powerful. In boot camp they taught us certain pressure points, certain ways to kill instantly and cleanly."

The playing cards lie unused on the table. "What are they?"

"What are what?" I ask.

"The pressure points."

I wave my hand in a dismissive gesture. "I ain't telling you."

She pouts. "Why not?"

"Tricks of the trade."

She flashes a sarcastic smile. "Then you're a killer by trade?"

I shrug. "I'm an ex-Marine. Draw your own conclusions."

The way she narrows her eyes at me now as she begins to quietly shuffle the cards makes me believe she's sending me a silent message, a telepathic valentine that says kill instead of love.

"Gin rummy it is," she says, dealing out the cards.

CHAPTER 19

Storm clouds gather in the dull gray October sky. The wind starts to whistle against the windowpanes. Nicole gets up and starts a fire in the fireplace with some dry kindling and old newspaper. When the blaze licks upward she tosses a log or two on the metal crib.

She sits down again opposite me and we finish the card game, neither of us saying much. I hear the crackle of the fire and the click of cards against her fingernail as she deals.

We don't really need to talk. I sense that a mental contract has been signed between us.

Evan returns from the shopping trip just about when we finish the card game. We have more champagne and a big dinner. We toast marshmallows while thunder booms in the distance and rain falls. When we have sex she treats me like a sheik and sort of ignores Evan, maybe making him jealous. That's not good. It would be a better strategy to soothe his ego and get him off guard. But she's calling the shots.

Later I conk out on the sofa, looking, I imagine, peaceful and content. But I sleep uneasily. Inside me gears are turning and meshing and the dream machine is going full blast. Well, I'm not exactly dreaming, am I? I'm plotting on the surface of sleep, sometimes plunging deep down in the well of unconsciousness and then resurfacing. Something's going on.

Sleep fits the pieces together. Sleep helps me to decide and to stick to my guns. As the rain patters outside the plan is seeping into my head like ink on a blotter. I always knew this time would come, this chance to make the big score. Everything in my life up to now must have been some sort of a limbering up exercise for this, the main event. Everything. Combat, the slammer, the booby hatch, all of it. Now it's payback time.

I dive under again and dream about making love to Nicole. I'm one of those people who remembers his dreams—every act, every scene in the drama. Then I relive the dream during the day and it gets so bad that sometimes I don't know which is which. It's an outlet for me, keeps me from going nuts. I cackle to myself.

I wake up with a crick in my neck from sleeping in an awkward position. It's still dark and rainy outside. I get up and shuffle to my bedroom upstairs where I immediately fall asleep again, this time like a baby.

At the crack of dawn I wake up again. I'm not feeling all that refreshed. I pad over to the bathroom, wait a few seconds for my hard-on to go down and then take a pee that would fill Lake Michigan. I give a shudder of satisfaction and go back and sit down on the bed.

I'm thinking about my new-found brother and I come to the conclusion that he's a softy and a patsy. I mean, he's always probing, asking questions about Violet and what kind of a dude our natural father might have been, and all that sort of crap. I keep telling him I couldn't give two farts in a windstorm about all that stuff but he doesn't seem to buy it. The old man was a son-of-a-bitch, that's for sure. A love-em-and-leave-em flyboy, I'll lay odds. A no-good, just like me. But Evan says, maybe not. Maybe they were in love, our parents, but he got killed in a combat mission in Korea before they could get hitched. Something like that.

I say, bullshit makes the grass grow tall.

I'm sure he was an Air Force man, though. I feel it in my gut. And I got vibes from Violet too, from her attitude toward the flyboys who came into our place. But I don't dwell on the subject, which is something Evan can't seem to understand. I'm not all that curious about our roots. I don't give a toot about past history; I got my eye on the future. And, for some reason, it gets my goat when he insists on talking about it. The other day he asked me if I wondered why she gave him up for adoption and kept me. Why it wasn't the other way around. I wanted to change the subject but he pressed it. He said, maybe that proves she loved me more.

"If she loved me more she would of kept you in that stinkhole roadside joint and given me to the fancy parents. Ever look at it that way?"

"That's a thought," he said.

"Anyhow I don't give a rat's ass about who loved who."

"Don't you? I thought everybody did."

"You thought wrong." I went to the refrigerator for a bottle of beer.

"Where's Violet now?" Evan asked.

"Dead, I expect." I drank. "But I really don't know. We lost touch about twenty years ago."

"So? What makes you think she's dead?"

"Her health wasn't none too good. She'd be close to seventy now. And she always smoked like a chimney and drank like a fish. Not to mention a few other bad habits. I figure she kicked the bucket."

"Doesn't the thought make you sad?"

"Nah. I got no heart."

"Do we look like Violet?"

"Not much. The blonde in her hair came out of a bottle. Her eyes were hazel. I guess she was okay-looking in her prime. But I didn't see much of her prime."

"No family resemblance, eh?"

"Not that I ever noticed—except for a streak of orneriness and a taste for the sauce."

The conversation went something like that, and I remember it gave me a headache. It even gives me a headache now, just thinking about it. Do I see a file of spiders trooping across the floor? I shake my head and smile, thinking about all the gooks, cons, psychos and drifters I have killed. Nicole's face appears in my mind and then it merges with a picture of Violet Plaine. Pretty soon this picture dissolves. I watch the progress of the spiders, now joined by centipedes and scorpions.

My eyelids feel heavy and my head's pounding like a bongo drum. I debate with myself about going back to sleep and I end up asking, what's the use? It occurs to me now that if I want things to run like a charm I may have to cut down on my drinking and such. All this booze, dope, food and sex after years of doing without have made me more than a little swinish. Now I need my wits about me. The question is, do I have the will power to cut down? I laugh aloud at myself and the sound echoes in the room. Then I'm quiet for a while. I look down at my bare toes. The nails need trimming. I do "this little piggy went to market . . ." I laugh again.

I stretch out again on the bed and let my mind dwell on the idea of erasing him. Will I have mixed feelings? I don't know. Not that I'm softhearted but I guess it does seem a little like killing a piece of yourself. Look at it another way, though: it's a way of being reborn, of making yourself whole again.

Hey, it's going to be a relief to finally get this monkey off my back, this feeling that half of me was always missing, that I was split down the middle from the beginning of my existence, making me only half a man. Maybe this twinship is the root cause of all my problems in life, all my false starts and fuck-ups. I just never knew how to fix the situation. I know now.

How will I do it? When and where? The questions buzz around in my brain like goddamn bumblebees. I hate doubts and questions and the need to plan things out. I'm no good at it. I like quick thinking, snap decisions, instinctive reactions. I'm a gunslinger at heart. I shoot from the hip and I make no excuses for it. But this requires a little strategy, a few blueprints. Yeah.

Through the glass doors leading to the terrace I look up at the sky. It's drizzling outside. I get up from the bed and stumble out onto the terrace. My bare feet feel cool on the wet quarry tiles. I look at the surrounding landscape, full of little pine trees and sand dunes that appear dull in the cloudy morning.

I spot him swimming in the pool, just under the rain-pocked surface of the water. He glides, my brother, sleek and quick. Suddenly, in a flash of inspiration, come the answers to my questions about where and how. I don't know, but there's a *rightness* about it. Predestination. The end must take place in the same kind of environment as the beginning. The back of my neck tingles. What's going on here? Why am I feeling so . . . ? Excited and sad at the same time.

I watch his wavy outline skim the green water and the old grudge surges within me. I realize I'm getting a second chance to win the fight that I lost ages and ages ago. His body knives through the pool and my eyes are glued to his right heel jutting out of the water.

He comes out of the water and lies naked by the side of the pool in the light rain. Then he sees me. He waves. I stare at him, my brother, my twin, my partner, my rival, my enemy, myself.

Meanwhile the party continues. Nicole stays apart from us most of the day, reading a book and preserving her energy for the evening's merrymaking, I guess. Evan and I shoot pool in the basement and I beat the pants off his ass. He's not too happy about it either. Well, screw him.

The sun starts to go down and the rain stops. We have cocktails on the deck, dinner by firelight, the same old routine. Am I getting jaded already? Afterwards, of course, Nicole puts us through our paces again, the sweet insatiable cunt. She gives me a beautiful blow job while he dicks her from the rear. Then we switch places. She acts like she never heard the expression, "Three's a crowd."

Later, with an evil grin, she goes to get a tape measure to compare our stiff dicks. I have to admit, what follows is a pretty funny scene. After playing coy for a minute or two she announces that we're "two pee-pees in a pod." Yuk, yuk. I glance over at my bro'. He doesn't seem amused.

Meanwhile she gives me plenty of reason to think that she's only stringing him along and would prefer to have me all by my lonesome.

In fact, once during a pause in the fun-and-games, she whispers in my ear that I really had him beat by a centimeter-and-a-half (that's a metric mile, when you come to think of it) but she didn't want to give him an inferiority complex. Hah! I can't imagine that stuck-up snob feeling inferior about anything. But you never know, do you?

I'm still drinking more than I should. I really can't help it. After such a long drought all the fountains have been turned on. Who could resist? In fact I start the ball rolling at breakfast, always spiking my coffee. What the hey. I can handle him even if I'm three sheets to the wind.

This morning we sit around the kitchen quietly. Evan

and I look very much alike, coincidentally barechested and both wearing pajama bottoms. We all have breakfast together, a cozy threesome. I have cold cereal with milk and sliced bananas. Soon Evan walks out on the deck and Nicole disappears for a while in the bathroom. I loiter around the kitchen, scratching my stubbled cheek and nursing the spiked java. I stretch and yawn.

A few minutes later she comes out of the john and walks over to me. In a low voice she says to me, "I'm going to the city tomorrow. The coast will be clear." She says it in a scheming tone. I look at her and narrow my eyes. She smiles thinly and her expression is kind of icy and bold. Now I'm positive what her message is.

After a second her tone becomes, like, flippant, as if she's afraid that the room is bugged or some such thing. She says, "With me out of the way you guys can become better acquainted."

"Sure," I say in a knowing voice. "Sure."

She sits down. She gives off a sour morning odor mixed with a fancy French perfume. After coffee we share a joint to wire us some more. She makes it clear that she doesn't want Evan to know she's smoking. She's being a naughty girl. He doesn't know she has any stuff.

Then she suggests that we go downstairs to play ping-pong while Evan's in the john. She's a pretty good player. Of course I'm distracted, watching her tits bounce under the tee shirt. Her secret weapon. So I lose the first game. She's fairly athletic; her coordination's good, her reflexes sharp, her body trim and agile. Still, I could beat her if I really bore down.

Both of us are flying high, of course, especially after the reefers. Well, one thing leads to another and now we're fucking on the floor right there in the game room. My left thigh hits up against the foot of the pinball machine. It's revved-up sex, wild and wooly. I pump her pretty good, top and bottom, and after she comes once or twice she seems very grateful and licks me all over, dwelling especially on the number 2 that I have tattooed on the left side of my belly. She keeps saying, "Yummy—two for the price of one" and weird stuff like that until she gets down to it, tonguing me from hairy root to purple crown while I am lying flat on my back with my hands laced behind my head, nice as you please. My breath begins to clog as her curly head bobs up and down and soon I come a second time, shooting jism all over my abdomen as she makes jawbreakers of my tingling balls.

She rolls over and gazes glassy-eyed at the ceiling. "I'm so glad we found you, Jason," she says in a very heartfelt way. "So glad."

The meaning is plain, especially after what she said to me about her going back to the city and the coast being clear. It's as if she was putting out a contract on him. I can take a hint. I'm just the man for the job.

While we were fooling around Evan painted a landscape on the deck. Not a bad job. I never had any talent in that direction, at least not that I am aware of. I would have discovered it in stir. A lot of guys get artsy-craftsy in the joint, I guess from the combination of solitude, hopelessness, anger and the need to escape reality. I didn't swing that way. I wonder if a person can be an artist of violence. I much preferred lifting weights, shooting hoops, kicking ass, more competitive pastimes. I was also always protecting my handsome backside from the cons who wanted to make me their wife, you know? But I didn't swing that way either. Not then, not now, not ever. You got that? Believe you me, I had to be pretty hard-boiled to convince some of the bruisers who had the hots for me to keep their paws off. When cupid's arrow hits those suckers they fall hard. But I managed to get the message out, right? I won't go into the grisly details.

I'm on the deck studying the landscape he has painted. I look at the real landscape, Nature's work, where a few clouds are banked on the horizon of the ocean, and I tell him, "It's beautiful. Very, very good."

He ducks his head a little. "It's nothing," he says and it's clear that he's not being modest, that he really doesn't think all that much of his painting. He's not fishing for compliments. "I just dashed it off to keep in shape, sort of." He turns and looks at me hard. "You know what I mean? I put nothing of my real self into it. Well—maybe not nothing. But very little. Very little."

I grunt and nod. "Yeah." I frown at the easel and tilt my head. "Still, it shows talent. At least I think so."

"Thanks," he says. He seems really touched.

"You're welcome."

He looks at me and I look at him. Mirror, mirror on the wall. Then we both look away, embarrassed.

That night Nicole fucks me to a frazzle while he just watches and jerks off. It's like she's giving me a going-away present, you know? And she's also giving me a clear message that she prefers me to him and that she wants to drink her fill of me, lick the plate before she has to leave. I swear, she's fucking me in an inspirational, courage-giving way. Not that I need any extra incentives. I'm not the kind of guy to get cold feet. I've been in some tough scrapes in the past, sure as shit. This operation will be no sweat for battle-scarred me.

The firelight carves nice clefts and valleys in her body. She gets on top now and plants her pussy square on my hot hammer. Oh, she moves nice.

Under her churning motions, I steal a glance at my brother across the room. He doesn't seem jealous at all. He's an odd duck. A dead duck too.

They leave me sleeping in front of the fire. Pretty soon I wake up again and start to think. Why do we think and brood about everything? It's such a waste of time and energy. I just have to steel myself to do it, plain and simple. Send him packing on his trip to eternity. Give him an early ticket, that's all. Why think twice about it? I couldn't ask for a sweeter setup. Once we're alone, hell, I could snuff him anytime, anywhere. I could just sneak up behind him, say, maybe while he's painting a picture or something, and do my Marine tricks on him. One, two, three. He won't know what hit him, poor sucker. I cackle to myself and harvest lint from between my toes.

Next question: do I have the stomach for it, especially in the case of a dude who looks exactly like me (not to mention the blood ties)? I laugh again.

Lying in bed, I make my mind a blank like I would do in 'Nam before a major battle or before going out on patrol in the mucky terrain the brass called "Eye Corps." I'll never forget the monotonous string of days of cold drizzle and fog, what the gooks called *crachin*. Then the numbing cold when the typhoon roared in from the sea and, on top of that, the hot dusty summers that parched you to a fucking pucker. I can still see the rocket fire flaring across the blue night sky when I would make my mind a blank, erasing every memory and every hope, every lust, every longing. Now the memories flood back. The Tet Offensive, January 1968. Four months of hell. In one day we lost three hundred grunts near Con Thien. The siege of Khe Sanh. The countryside looked like a moonscape.

Make it blank. Erase it.

I hear the jeep cough and start up. But I don't bat an eye or move a muscle. This is the day. I listen to the grinding of tires on gravel and I realize that Evan is taking Nicole to the train station and soon I and my brother will be alone. An engraved invitation, if I ever saw one.

I toss and turn for a while. Then I get up and walk to the john to brush my teeth. I glance at my mug in the glass, taking the toothbrush out of my mouth and straightening up like a ramrod for inspection. The fever sores have all but disappeared and I think I look pretty good, except for the signs of too much drinking that show in the redness of the eyes and the dark rings around them. But I still look better than I have in a long time. It must be the steady diet of good nutritious food. I turn my head this way and that. I could easily pass for Evan Beck now. Any day of the week.

I go back to the bedroom and start to get dressed. How do you get dressed to kill, I wonder? I chuckle. That depends on the weather, doesn't it? I switch on the radio and listen to some Country and Western.

Doubts flash and I frown. I don't like to analyse things too much. If I make up my mind to do something, I don't look backwards. I plunge right in. If I fall on my face, those are the breaks. I pay the piper.

I lay clothes out on the bed: blue cords, plaid flannel shirt, striped fisherman's sweater, white sweat socks. I run my hands over the fine material. They're mine. I put them on. As I lace up a pair of Reeboks I wonder again if I can fill my twin brother's shoes in more ways than just in the sack where I already know I've got him outclassed. I don't wonder especially hard, just a little. I consider again if I could take up his acting career. Why should I, though? I'll let Nicole support me. She must be loaded with dough. Anyway, it doesn't pay to plan too far ahead; that much the school of hard knocks has taught me. I hear the radio say that it's forty-five degrees outside, going up to sixty.

I go downstairs to the living room and find some paper clips in an old pine desk and I play with them for about a half hour, linking them together and taking them apart, lining them up like toy soldiers. I enjoy it. It takes my mind off things.

I go to the kitchen and brew coffee. I sit there drinking and make my mind a blank again. A fog rolls in from the sea and blankets the house. I hear the jeep come up the driveway.

PART THREE

His Own Funeral

And when I died, the neighbors came
And buried brother John.

—HENRY SAMBROOKE LEIGH
The Twins

CHAPTER 20

*H*aving to attend the funeral has certainly crimped my sybaritic Saturday routine, which I invariably launch by brunching at the South Street Seaport (poached eggs *à la Reine* with truffles, raspberries and champagne, *café au lait)* and then follow by having an all-day session at the Ariadne Institute (manicure, pedicure, facial peel, full leg and bikini waxing, body massage and bust treatment). Ah the sacrifices one must make to portray the grieving widow!

The service *in memoriam* Evan Beck is held on a pristinely sunny day in the reddish-brown sandstone Episcopal Church in Greenwich Village where Evan and I were married (gown by de la Renta, of course) and into which we afterward rarely ventured since, clearly, we are not the church-going kind. Weddings and funerals in gloomy gothic are quite enough, thank you. Stained glass is not my style.

I'm very content, though. Everything seems to have gone without a hitch, I reflect, as I file into the first pew. The cops fell for the scenario hook, line and lure. After a routine autopsy I had the body cremated and the ashes scattered in the Hudson River. I told all and sundry that this was the way Evan would have wanted it. Then I invited a smattering of (insincere, I'm sure) mourners to this service on the day after the cremation.

I sit down and glance around the church. Not exactly SRO, I observe, arching a pencilled eyebrow. Evan had few friends and even fewer close relatives, none in New York. The mourners fill only the first two mahogany pews of the side chapel. I chuckle under my breath and lace my hands demurely in my lap. Why do I refer to him in the past tense?

I cast my jaded eyes around again and primp the tight curls of hair at the nape of my sleek cygneous neck. Nobody needs to tell me how exquisite I look today, or how absolutely right my clothes are: a navy blue wool suit by one of those new Japanese designers (I can never pronounce the names), a matching campaign style hat that fits snugly over my short hair, a black mesh veil that mutes the understated solemnity of my graceful expression, a sparkler by Harry Winston pinned to my lovely breast—all wreathed by a whiff of Passion from Elizabeth Taylor, chosen consciously for its incongruity to the setting. I should have been the actor rather than Evan.

To my right sits *Maman*, Dr. Mathilde Roche, spidery elegant as usual, composed and proud, her chilly blue eyes scrollworked with wrinkles, registering every nuance of her surroundings. Next to her sits Mitchell Rosen, Evan's agent, a fidgety man in his late fifties who has taken the trouble to wear a black tie and dark gray suit over his pear-shaped bulk. Even though the climate inside the church is cool and damp, he has to keep mopping the sweat from his brow, using a large blue handkerchief. Sitting at the end of the pew, holding hands, are Rachel and Ken Boardman, a young couple who live in our building. We sometimes socialize with them by going to a movie or a restaurant but they hardly can be called intimate friends of ours. This loveydovey pose they assume in public makes me chuckle. I've heard chapter and verse of their vituperative, knock-down, drag-out domestic disputes even through the thick plaster walls of our Mercer Street building and, believe you me, the language would make a drill sergeant blush and the content could provide running scripts for five sordid soap operas. I know for a fact that he runs around doing a fair imitation of a cordless screw driver, drilling everything that isn't nailed down, while she gets her pork regularly from a local bartender with hair on his forehead. Mr. and Mrs. Cleaver, they ain't, despite their public posturing. Ken is Evan's tennis and squash rival. Or *was,* I suppose I have to say now. Despite the couple's *grand guignol* relationship I always found their company about as lively and entertaining as watching a two buck haircut, but I tolerated them for Evan's sake. I'm so kind and self-sacrificing it's a wonder, really, that my name has never been submitted for canonization.

The second pew is occupied by a handful of actors, actresses, directors and designers who worked with Evan over the years and read of his death either in the trades or in the squib of an obit that appeared in one edition of Saturday's *Times.* His middling stage, movie and television career earned him on his death very little publicity. I hope the poor dear didn't notice. He has such a tender ego.

The obit might also have attracted the sparse gathering of peripheral onlookers who fill the rear section of the chapel. It's a ragtag group and I don't examine it too closely.

I hear the windy strains of an organ. A young curate, balding and bushy-bearded, lifts his skirts and steps up to the pulpit to deliver the eulogy. I cross my legs at the ankles and fuss again with the crisp curls of hair clustering at my neck. The altar behind the priest bristles with flowers—gladioluses, lilies-of-the-valley, roses—all very bright and cheerful. The priest, I'm sure, never met the subject of his little sermon and knows only the bare outlines of his life so the eulogy is likely to have a general and impersonal quality. He begins to talk about my dear departed *mari*, my sweet *bouton-d'or*, keying the theme to the acting profession, trying to be ever so clever by drawing his imagery from stagecraft. Sometimes I wish that sermons were reviewed in the daily tabloids under a rating system—like ranging from five haloes for very inspirational to one halo for totally insipid. Then perhaps these studs who wear their collars backwards would take as much care with the language and substance of their sermons as they seem to do with their silly costumes and voodoo ceremonies. Ah well, grin and bear it.

The priest rambles on. I notice the toes of jogging sneakers peeking out from under his cassock. His voice is high-pitched, chirpy.

"In life Evan Beck played many roles," he's saying. "But now he stands, stripped of all masks, whether of comedy or of tragedy, before his divine Maker." He pauses here for dramatic effect, gripping the edges of the lectern with his pink fingers. "We've all heard the expression, 'An actor prepares.' He prepares, as we all must prepare, for the final and most important role on the stage of our existences— that of beggar before the throne of God, seeking not applause or critical acclaim, not curtain calls or Oscars or Tonys or Emmys, but seeking life everlasting in His sight and in His favor." He pauses again, rubbing together his plump hands and scanning the faces of the mourners. Does he observe my expression of *ennui total*, the overgrown choir boy? His voice rises slightly as he says, "Let us pray that the soul of our beloved brother, Evan, rests now in the loving hands of Our Lord Jesus Christ; that his soul, free now from the mortal obligation to impersonate a suffering, earthbound thing, flies to the bosom of the Lord. May he rest in peace, Amen."

"Amen," echoes the congregation.

I give him no more than a halo and a half.

Dr. Roche, at my side, sketches a frown. Mitch Rosen mops his brow. Ken Boardman stifles a yawn.

The organ music brays louder. As the service concludes I examine my painted fingernails and scoff inwardly at the idea of eternity, at this sacred sense of a timeless world where spirits dwell in a blinding sort of light. What a cosmic joke, really! Self-love is my only religion and my body is my temple. My icons are money and things of the flesh— I won't mince words or try to kid anybody. Take it or leave it.

The priest's nasal chants and the swell of the organ provide background noise for my profane thoughts, which range now to the swimming pool on Fire Island where Jason made his hasty exit from time. I feel a little sad about it. Oh, I'm not exactly going to turn into a keening old crow of a mourner, but—brief as the liaison was—I will miss that sex-starved stumblebum and our cozy little household of three.

What is it that the organist is playing? Bach? Vivaldi? A baroque piece, in any case. It reminds me of a gurgling brook, of water.

I'm usually not the reflective type but I've been thinking about how odd it is that his life ended as it began, struggling in a pool against his brother, his rival of forty years standing. First it was a pool filled with amniotic fluid, then chlorinated water. At issue were matters of mirror-image quality: who would be the firstborn? Who would be the first to die?

Well, I conclude, as organ music fills the chapel, It's over now and the scheme worked like a charm. So far, at least. I gnaw on my painted lower lip. I ask myself, why then do I have this creeping feeling of unease?

I really have no reason to worry. Evan is just playing it smart, lying low, being extra cautious. That's it, of course. But why is it so hard for me to imagine him engaging in all these cloak-and-dagger activities? He's an actor, after all, playing the supreme role of his life. I have no reason to worry at all.

With a flurry of coughing and a rustle of clothing, the mourners rise to their feet as the service ends. I walk out of the pew and down the center aisle toward the rear of the church. I try not to smile at the simpering faces of all the clucks who are watching the beautiful widow like hawks, whispering to each other behind their hands. My eyes are limpid and tearless, but I don't avert them, don't try to put on an act of inconsolability. It would be out of character. I first look straight ahead and then side to side.

I catch a glimpse of him in the rear of the church. My step falters for an instant and my stomach gets knotted up, but I try to keep a calm expression.

Once outside on the dappled sidewalk I begin to collect my emotions and thoughts. I picture him again. He was slouched in the last pew, wearing a sad and cynical smirk. His complexion had an unhealthy greenish tinge. He had a stubbly beard and wore dark glasses and the camouflage jacket—that much I took in. Around his head was wrapped a large white bandage.

The mourners, so-called, are standing around chatting with each other and offering me condolences. Rachel Boardman makes some *outré* remark about Evan's "cremains." I mutter perfunctory replies as my brain programs what I have just seen in the rear of the church.

Surely it was Evan. He has done a very cunning thing, and a natural one, when you come to think of it. He has disguised himself as what his brother was—a homeless derelict. What could be more commonplace, anonymous and faceless on the streets of New York, than these spectral unfortunates whom hardly anyone really looks at anyway? It's a perfect ploy. I'm surprised I didn't think of it myself.

Yet doubt nibbles at me. It is too convincing a masquerade. I don't believe that Evan is that clever an actor.

Mitch Rosen is saying something to me that passes right over my head but I flash him a *papier-mâché* smile and nod politely. My mother, who stands three inches taller than I, hovers protectively by my side, holding my elbow. I cringe at her reptilian touch. She's been treating me gingerly since the news of Evan's purported death, causing me to wonder what she has up her sleeve. If the old rattler thinks I'm going to move in with her or share the loot, she's got another think coming.

People keep yapping at me but I don't hear most of what they're saying, especially in the hubbub of traffic and the squeals of children being let out of a nursery school across the street.

I hear Ken Boardman say, "Did I understand right, you're selling the loft?"

My hands wring an embroidered handkerchief. "Yes. I've already listed it with a broker." The question prompts pleasant thoughts of riches on the horizon. I think I'll buy a Maserati in France. And maybe a power boat, a small one. I picture myself downing daiquiris in St. Tropez.

"The memories associated with living in the loft are too painful, I'm sure," my mother volunteers with a phoney frown of sympathy. She looks like she's having the time of her life, the faker. I suddenly notice her hair: since when has it been auburn?

"Where will you live?" Rachel Boardman asks. I glance at her. She's wearing a dated denim dress. I hunch my fashionably padded shoulders. "I've pretty much decided to leave the country. I'm going to wipe the slate clean, I think. Live in the South of France for a while."

My mother's hand tenses on my elbow, but she doesn't say anything.

I glance sidelong at the front steps of the church. Is he still inside? Did he slip out another door? Yes, I tell myself, he doesn't want to be recognized. But why was he foolish enough to come at all? It's not like Evan to take unnecessary risks. I guess he couldn't resist the temptation to attend his own funeral.

"Back to your roots, eh?" continues Rachel.

"Something like that," I say with an artificial smile, using curt answers to chill her obvious attempts to become chummy.

"Damn shame about Evan," says Mitchell, swabbing the deep folds in his neck. I sniff the air and stand back a pace in reflexive fear that the man's *gaucherie* might be contagious. He wags his unkempt head. "Such an athletic guy too. Just goes to show, you never know in this world, do you? I always thought I would go first, with my bum ticker." He stuffs the handkerchief in his pocket. Despite his efforts sweat glistens on his deeply creased face. "He was a fine actor, a fine actor."

Dr. Roche arches an eyebrow at the florid-faced man and looks into the distance with disdain.

Mitchell doesn't notice. "He was on the brink of a breakthrough in his career, too. I felt it in my bones."

"Oh, indeed?" says my mother, not bothering to conceal her skepticism.

Mitchell checks his wrist watch. He says, "Well, I must be toddling off." He starts nervously at the screech of a child at play across the street.

Dr. Roche looks relieved. She raises a bony hand in the air. "Everybody's invited to lunch at my place," she tells the gathering. "I live right around the corner on West

Tenth. Salmon *Mousseline Chantilly. Meringues Glacées.''* She looks expectantly at the faces of the group. Some, including Mitch Rosen, make excuses and leave. The freeloading Boardmans and three other acquaintances accept the invitation. I guess there's no way I can wriggle out of it.

Under a dazzling sun we walk through the decorative streets of Greenwich Village to my mother's apartment, chatting amiably. Dry leaves crunch under our shoes. Although my demeanor seems relaxed, my mind of course is racing over possibilities and foreseeing problems, considering alternative actions and potential obstacles to carrying out my original scheme. Despite the heat of the sun I feel a chill scuttling down my spinal cord.

CHAPTER 21

I begin the hour by working on my "glutes," as André calls the gluteus muscles of the buttocks. I do squats, dead lifts and lunges, eight reps each. But before very long, I'm pooped and I put the barbell down with a thud. I guess I'm showing the effects of all that high living in Davis Park and my progressive resistance techniques have regressed a tad. I'd better take a plate off and work my way back into shape. Bernard McFadden, pictured in a poster taped on the wall before me, seems to be glaring at me.

I take two five-pound plates off and begin again. No sweat, this time.

Now for the bustline. I start with arm circles, fifteen in each direction. Then I lie on the bench for some dumbbell flys and flat pullovers. Now I'm ready for the leg curl machine, also designed to tighten up my sweet ass.

I lie on my stomach, making sure that the backs of my ankles come into contact with the pads of the movement arm. As I begin the leg curls I think about what happened at the funeral service and gloom descends over me. As I slowly lower my legs and feel my butt contract I reflect that if I don't hear from Evan soon I'm going to have to take some kind of action, plot some moves. I pout. Damn it, I detest being kept in the dark and I loathe having to alter my plans. I wish I had a dog because I feel like kicking one. I suppose that's one of the things pumping iron's good for —letting off steam. But it's not nearly as soul-satisfying as hurting a living thing.

Pumping iron also makes me as horny as a grub-eating toad.

Where is he, anyhow?

My Achilles' tendons feel sore, another effect, I assume, of my sloth and gluttony and lust at the seashore. Ah, the seven deadly sins! How many of them have I fallen prey to? Each and every one, thank goodness. That's why I exercise so hard; the hair shirt is not my style. I got my belly full of self-castigation, thank you, in that flagellant convent school *ma mère* had the nerve to commit me to when I was too young to do anything about it. The idea that being sentenced to that institution might curb my budding appetite for erotic activity was ludicrous. Poor benighted *maman*. For a Frenchwoman and a physician to boot, she certainly lacks sophistication in matters of the flesh. Of course my two years at Saint Agatha's did not cure me of the disease we used to call "boy-craziness." It merely opened up new and unconventional vistas for exploration by an eager young *conquistadora* like myself.

As I continue the curls my eyes are riveted on a large color poster of "Ms. America," Laura Coombes. Now my goddamn "glutes" are killing me, as well as my "pecks." Oh well, no pain, no gain.

When the nuns failed, I reflect as I walk over to the pullover machine, she took a new tack and tried sending me to a therapist. Naturally, I recall with a smirk, I seduced the shrink. And with all his jabbering and moaning about professional ethics, he was a pushover. One minute he's

posing probing questions about my absentee father and before you know it, he's probing me. I saw him twice a week
for six months before he began to bore the beejesus out of
me. I stretched it out longer than I really wanted to because
it gave me wicked pleasure to have mother fork over a
C-note a session for him to poke me regularly. When I finally gave him his walking papers, the big, tweedy, sono-
rous-voiced dumbbell bawled like a baby. I had to laugh. I
should have put him on the couch.

My father is another one for the books, I think as I sit
down at the pullover machine and fasten the seat belt
around my sylphlike waist. I push the foot pedal, bringing
the elbow pads into position. What a classic case study he
makes (and, by extension, so do I!).

Emile Roche, my father, was a boot manufacturer in
Dreux who became very rich in the postwar years. We lived
what I dimly recall as a very decorous and serene existence
in that lovely provincial Norman town, full of ruined med-
ieval castles, gothic spires and lush manicured parks. The
house teemed with servants, gleamed with silverware and
firelight, sparkled with crystal and with lively conversation
from a stream of well-groomed, well-educated and well-
heeled guests. It was so long ago, it seems unreal now, and
perhaps the gauziness of the memory makes me romanti-
cize the reality. But I don't think so.

In any case it didn't last. I move my elbows vigorously,
working the pullover machine. No, my mother did not surprise my father boffing the parlor maid. She had a mustache
and, in any event, that kind of thing would have been easy
to overlook. What happened? Exactly—she caught him
buggering the manservant, a young Corsican who, I remember, had perpetual five-o'clock shadow, striking green eyes
and no scruples whatsoever.

So our Dresden china world was shattered.

It was regarded as a *scandale*, of course, and Dr. Mathilde

Roche, never one to shrink on the field of battle, sounded the trumpets of retribution. She got a widely-publicized church annulment, a large cash settlement and much sympathy from the matrons of Dreux. She whisked me off to Paris. I was seven years old. Soon father's business suffered, then failed. He was left nearly penniless and, I suppose, broken in spirit, although I could never confirm the fact with my own eyes for I never saw him again.

Plenty of material there for the amateur shrinks, eh?

Pearls of perspiration form on my brow and neck. I unstrap myself from the contraption and go over to the fridge for some Gatorade. I take long swigs straight from the bottle and, when I'm refreshed, I head for the double chest machine. Except for an elastic cotton headband and star-shaped diamond earrings I am as naked as a jay bird, my preference when exercising.

As I work the machine with both arms I continue thinking about my checkered past. When I was eight we emigrated to New York where my maternal grandmother lived and where mother secured a teaching post at New York University Medical Center, specializing in neurology. Mother never remarried, spending her meager emotional bank account on me, to my eternal regret. Of course I was born with a streak of something that was probably inherited from my father—I don't know what to call it, I'll leave the nomenclature to the experts—that no amount of convent schooling and prim and proper upbringing could eradicate.

I make no bones about my selfishness and hedonism and all my other personality traits that some people might consider flaws; I myself don't consider them defects or even good points, for that matter. I'm a rare bird, I believe: a genuinely amoral person. That's the conclusion I would come to if I bothered my head about such things, which I usually don't.

So why am I doing it now, I wonder, grunting through the exercise? Because of Evan, I suspect.

I never cared a whit for anybody in the world except myself until he came along, with his handsome mug and sugary ways. Then I cared. A whit. I still might not have married him if he hadn't been a potential matinee idol, his star on the rise at the time. To be blunt, I had visions of a beachfront villa in Malibu, a lodge in Aspen, snowfalls in any season. But it was not exactly in the cards. Oh, we haven't had to collect green stamps during our life together. I don't mean to paint too bleak a picture. And it did help enormously that we were so compatible in the sack. But we never reached the peaks I had envisioned.

That's why I was so happy when Jason dropped from the sky.

I breathe evenly and push the parallel bars all the way forward. I guess I started tiring of Evan about two years ago when he left for Malaga to shoot a movie. Instead of missing him terribly I remember feeling liberated during his three-month absence. The leash, long as it was, had begun to chafe.

I release the bars and relax my muscles. Should I go back to the free weights or have I had enough? I'll do one cycle of leg extensions on the machine, then cool down and call it quits.

I climb into position on my back and begin the exercise, careful to control the rhythm of my breathing. This exercise, requiring me to bring my knees to my chest and then raise the thingamajig with the force of my feet by extending my legs, always has a particularly erotic effect on me. Now, as I perform the cycle, dew forms on my rosebud.

Mmmmm. It was wonderful having a matched set for a while, I reflect, focusing my senses on my shimmering flower. Quite wonderful. But all good things must come to an end and Jason's usefulness transcended the sexual.

Thinking about him reminds me again of how clever Evan's disguise was. I wish he would contact me so I can finally get this over with. I continue to pump the machine, trying through physical activity to erase negative thoughts from my mind. The petals open and close.

Soon I am so wrapped up in these pleasurable sensations that I don't even hear him come in. How stealthy he is, how feathery of foot for one so powerfully built. Of course the wall-to-wall industrial carpeting and the soundproofing of the studio help to cover his approach.

I'm feeling suddenly more energetic and I decide to do another cycle of leg extensions. Before long I enter a state of euphoria, a natural high that sometimes eddies over me while exercising. I surrender to its warm ebb and flow, oblivious to everything around me.

The swirl of his cool tongue on my vulva brings me back to a sweet reality. I whimper softly and squirm slightly, locking my hands behind my knees. "There you are," I sigh.

He surfaces for a moment. "It looked so inviting, I couldn't resist."

"How dare you take advantage of a grieving widow," I say mockingly.

He laughs and descends again.

I reach around to cup his ears. I untense my muscles, part my legs, and ride the chariot of his expert tongue. "Oh, André," I moan. "Yes, André!"

"That's the first time I've cooled down by heating up," I say afterwards.

"Not the first time at all," he reminds me, regaining his feet and licking his lips (the satyr!). Of course he's right. From the very beginning our relationship has been based on a spicy mixture of sex and exercise. With some people it's food or drugs that help ignite the fire. With André and me it's pumping iron. And food. And drugs.

"Care for some music?" he asks, walking over to the sound system and riffling through some compact discs. We are in his top-floor loft on Spring Street. Sun streams through the skylight above him, bronzing his dark curls and giving his sharp features a saturnine cast.

I stretch and say, "Sure."

He inserts a reggae number. "How about a joint?" he asks.

I shrug and say, "Why not? I've earned it."

He nods and goes over and gets the stuff out of his knapsack, hanging on a peg by the door. "How was the funeral?" he asks.

"Let's not discuss unpleasant subjects," I say.

His bushy mustache curls upward in a smile as he offers me the first toke. "Here we are still doing pot," he says, "in today's prohibitionist atmosphere."

I snort and say, "I'm just an old-fashioned girl. You know that."

"Yeah," he says, chuckling to himself. "Sure." He takes a puff himself.

I study his biceps, rippling with muscles, networked with bulging veins. A lot of women don't like the exaggerated muscularity of the bodybuilder, the Olympian look. I can really get into it, especially as a change of pace. Getting pronged by André is like getting screwed by a steel robot—there's a mindless and relentless quality about it that's oddly appealing to me. I don't analyse it too closely. I'm interested in sex, not cybernetics.

"Another hit?" he asks.

I shake my head and lean back on the couch, feeling the buzz. "I'm cool for now."

"Yeah," he says again.

André, of course, is a card-carrying airhead. That's a major part of his appeal.

He begins to massage the inside of my thigh. With a mock pout I slap his hand.

He looks wounded.

I bounce energetically up from the leather couch. "Have to run, sugar mouth."

"What's the damn hurry?"

"Duty calls," I say, gathering up my belongings. "You think it's easy acting the part of the grieving widow?"

"Geez," he says. "Have a little respect. He was your husband, after all."

I sway to the Afro-Caribbean beat as I shimmy into the miniskirt. I bat my eyes in a mockery of remorse and say, "Through my fault, through my fault, through my most grievous fault," burlesquing the Act of Contrition of my girlhood. I think to myself, if he only knew the half of it . . .

Buckling my stilettos from a standing position, I present a blossoming rear which he fondles abstractedly. "Please," I say, "unhand my glutes. Do you want me to fall on my face?"

From the couch he looks up at me, peering hard. "Have you ever?"

I straighten up. "Have I ever what, sweet nuts?"

"Have you ever fallen on your face?"

I produce makeup paraphernalia from my handbag and begin to do up my face, using the full-length mirror that André uses for posing. "You ask that in a hopeful tone of voice," I observe, starting on my eyes.

He shrugs. "Not really. But you haven't answered the question."

I turn and look at him, widening my newly-mascaraed eyes. Then I say, "Not yet, my little demigod. Not yet."

CHAPTER 22

*A*s I walk home from André's studio I try to ignore the admiring glances and puerile comments of the bozos who follow the clack of my Charles Jourdan heels and the bobbing of my bottom down the graffiti-filled streets of SoHo. Sex has sharpened my senses and electrified my nerves, but my mind is occupied with deadly serious matters.

I'd like to get this thing over with, but my hands are tied until he makes contact. The situation is far from amusing. I like being in the driver's seat, that's pretty clear. And I detest being kept waiting. Apprehension only fuels my anger.

Heading south on Mercer Street, past loading platforms and alleys filled with bulging trash bags, I turn my thoughts to André and his neolithic charms. I mull over whether I should continue the affair that has gone on for almost a year now, a fairly long run for me. He's often handy to have around as he proved just a few minutes ago. But he may prove troublesome in the long run. I sense a disconcerting streak of possessiveness in the man. He could turn out to be even more proprietary than Evan.

Poor Evan. Much as he tried to be liberal-minded about it, he frowned on my inclination to have a fling or two. And he himself seemed to have no desire to stray despite, obviously, many opportunities. So I considered discretion the better part of valor and kept him in the dark about André. After all, why go looking for trouble?

I reach the loft building and fit the key into the lock of the front door. Before entering I look around at the chic squalor of the street. I'll be glad to leave this dump, I conclude. The charms of Bohemian living have begun to fade. I miss having a wetback or two to carry my packages and take out the garbage for me. From now on, when I'm not pumping iron, I vow to lift nothing heavier than my Gold Card.

Of course Evan would always take care of the chores, the little puppy dog. But the time came when I began to feel smothered by him even though my affection for him had not diminished. Needless to say, the way his career began to sputter didn't help matters.

I get the mail and riffle through the stack. Nothing from the insurance company yet. I suppose it's still much too early for the payoff. Let's see—Bloomie's is having a sale on lingerie; some slant-eyed wimp is running for the City Council; another real estate broker wants to list the loft. Ho hum. I half-hoped for a letter or postcard from him. But no dice. I sigh and head for the freight elevator.

As I sail upward in the noisy contraption I check my horoscope in a fashion magazine that came in the mail. It should come as no surprise that I'm a Virgo. I hold my forefinger under the subheading and read: "A deeper awareness of social issues in the next few days can transform you into a successful fund-raiser for your favorite charity or political or social group." That's a hoot! It's common knowledge who my favorite charity is. Let's see what it has to say about my pending relationship to filthy lucre. "While your moon ruler is eclipsed toward the end of the month you may decide to travel abroad, marking a significant change in your financial fortunes." That sounds promising. But is it a change for the better or a change for the worse, pray tell? What about my love life? "You will soon renew a fiery relationship with an old flame." I close the magazine with a frown.

I open the door to my apartment and switch on the Murano lamp by the elevator. I collapse on the sofa and remove my shoes. I suddenly feel hunger pangs but I'm too lazy to do anything about them. If Evan were here I would only have to snap my fingers and he would quickly concoct a scrumptious meal. It's funny how I still think of him with fondness. Well, why not? There's no reason to take these matters personally.

I sigh and rouse myself to fix a snack. Then I drink two glasses of Evian water, completing my daily quota of six glasses. I take a quick shower and crawl between the sheets, taking the fashion magazine with me. I flip through it, absorbing a hazy montage of pretty pouts, hollow cheekbones, sleek legs and sultry poses, but none of the fashions really register. I'd like to take a nap before deciding where to go for dinner but I toss and turn, unable to fall asleep.

What's come over me anyhow? I'm not the type to worry and reflect so much. I think about how I had been waiting for a graceful and convenient exit from my life with Evan when the twin surfaced, a gift from the gods. I didn't see it as the solution to all my problems right away. At first I just saw it as a way for me and Evan to get out of our financial hole by collecting the insurance money. It took a little while longer before the whole plan dawned on me, before I realized that I was being presented with a golden opportunity not only to become rich but also to become free.

I hurl aside the magazine and lace my hands behind my head. I stare at the ceiling of embossed tin. After all, I figure, there was no way in hell that they could pin anything on me. Officially he would be dead already.

I am awakened from the nap by the jangle of the telephone. I bolt up in bed and grope for the receiver. I always thought I was unflappable, but obviously my nerves are frayed.

"Hullo?"

"Hello," he says.

I'm startled. It sounds like him. But I'm hesitant to mention the name in case it isn't. So I ask, "Who is this?"

"Three guesses," he says.

I frown as my ears prickle. This is no time for coyness. "Is it you?" I ask over the shoals of my breath.

"Yes."

"It's about time! Where the hell have you been?"

"Taking care of business." He pauses. "I did what you wanted me to do."

I puzzle over the sound of his voice. It seems changed. Of course, I reflect, he's been through a kind of *auto-da-fé* that would be likely to transform almost anybody. "You shouldn't have come to church," I say in a mildly scolding tone. "You took an unnecessary risk."

"So. You saw me?"

"I'm not blind, pizza pie. You know I never miss a trick."

"Don't you?"

I'm starting to fume. Why does he keep asking me these inane questions? "If someone had recognized you," I say, "We'd be up shit's creek without a paddle right now."

"I guess I wasn't thinking straight."

I hesitate before asking, "What happened to your head?"

"He bashed me."

"Brother Dearest?"

"Who else? No problem, though. It's already healing."

I'm struck by a distressing thought. "Who dressed the wound?" I ask. "I hope you didn't see a doctor."

"Nah. I wrapped it myself. Don't worry."

My suspicions, at first hazy, now take definite shape. Suppose, just suppose, that Jason somehow survived the attempt on his life and it really was Evan whose ashes I scattered to the four winds and the seven seas? While Evan and I were hatching the plot to kill Jason, could I somehow have led Jason to believe that I wanted him to kill Evan? I suddenly remember the time I mistook Jason for Evan and mentioned something to the effect that the coast was clear.

I rub my chin. Could Jason have interpreted the remark to mean that I wanted him to do away with Evan? It's possible. He wasn't screwed on all that tightly and, besides, I gave him plenty of reason to think that I rather enjoyed his company, even that I might prefer him to Evan. Farfetched, I conclude, but worth considering.

The question swells inside me, begging to be voiced. But for some reason I suppress it. Instead I ask, "Where are you now?"

He doesn't reply immediately. Rather he observes, "At the funeral yesterday. Nobody cried." He chuckles, incongruously amused.

"What do you expect?" I say. "People are heartless bastards. You should know that by now."

"You didn't cry either."

"I'm not the actor, honey. I can't cry on cue." I take the phone over to the wicker chair and collapse into it. I put my feet up on an ottoman and cross my ankles. I'm trying to relax physically in order to take control of the situation emotionally and intellectually. For once in my life I must learn to be totally self-reliant.

"Where are you?" I ask again.

"Not far. At some fleabag in the East Village. When can we get together?"

"Have you got any cash?"

"Some but not much. That's one of the reasons I wanted to see you."

I feel a pang of uncertainty. I hear the dim blare of a car horn on his end of the line. "We don't want to blow this thing at this stage of the game."

He presses the matter. "I'm dying to see you," he declares huskily.

I hear the groan of the freight elevator cranking up. Another tenant must be using it. I suddenly have a brainstorm. "Tell you what," I say, "—have you got enough cash to get to Davis Park? I could join you out there the day after tomorrow. It's a perfect place for you to keep out of sight and we're certain not to be disturbed."

"Yeah. I guess I've got enough money."

"Bring some clean clothes too. Take the train and the water taxi. There are plenty of provisions in the house. And the place is even more deserted now than before. Hardly anybody but the sea gulls visit this late in the year."

"You'll come tomorrow?"

"The day after tomorrow. I've got to wrap some things up here."

"Okay," he says in a disappointed tone. After a pause he adds, "I can't wait to get my hands on you."

Hmmm. I hope that remark had a sexual connotation. I get up from the chair and pace the hardwood floors, trailing the long telephone cord. "Take the next train out," I suggest. "You'll be a trillion times more comfortable in the beach house than in some roach-trap hotel." I take my purse out of the closet and fish out a film canister filled with grass. I roll a jay, cradling the phone between my ear and shoulder. I fumble for matches. "Hold on," I say. "I'm rolling a number." Come into my arms, Mary Jane, and give me the courage to ask the question. I light the reefer and frown at the phone.

"One thing I don't understand," he says.

"What's that?"

"Why did you cremate me?"

I give a startled laugh, a nervous reaction born of alarm. I toke twice and my senses buzz. The stuff works fast. "What . . . what do you mean?" I ask. "What's the difference. Would you rather have been buried?"

"I'd rather have lived," he says.

A palpable silence hangs between us. My throat feels clogged with cotton. I breathe deeply, gathering myself. Finally I ask, "Who the hell are you?"

"Who am I?"

"You heard me."

"I'm Evan Beck."

But this reply is essentially ambiguous. Does he mean that he's really Evan Beck who has killed Jason Plaine? Or does he mean that he is Jason Plaine who has killed Evan Beck and has assumed his victim's identity? Whoever he is, the rest of the world must continue to believe that Evan Beck is dead or my scheme will fail.

"Remember this," I say in a firm voice. "Evan Beck is dead. His ashes are in the Hudson River." My voice rises, now grainy with fear. "Remember—he's dead!"

I hear the sound of my own breathing and the gurgle of his nearly silent laughter.

I stare at the phone for a long time before hanging up. I feel like I'm living some kind of existentialist joke, a crisis of identity and a saga of alienation come to life. Or come to death.

I chew a fingernail and snuff out the joint in an ashtray. Right now I need paranoia producers like a hole in the head. My thinking must be crystal clear, my emotions under tight rein. I suddenly recall Evan's idea about the tags on twins getting switched at birth. Could this have something to do with his present muddle over his identity? But it was only conjecture on his part, not fact.

I go over to the window and search for answers in the dark autumn sky. I think about how they were once a single living organism, combining the essences (the souls?) of two persons before the egg divided. And now who's who? It's the question twins are always asked by smart alecks. Who's who? The question is a deep and fundamental one.

I must get dressed. I go over to the big French Provincial armoire and search through the hangers. A chain of gaudy possibilities keeps clanking through my mind. The caller whom I just spoke to is really Evan but his mind has snapped as a result of having killed his own twin brother. It makes sense. He was not the murdering kind, Evan. So his rubber band broke after he did the bidding of his Lady Macbeth. Now the poor sap doesn't know who the hell he is.

The other possibility is that Jason killed Evan, thinking that I put him up to it. And now he wants to take Evan's place. Or maybe he thinks he *is* Evan. Mental stability was never Jason's strong suit.

My head's reeling from all this. I lay out on the bed a pair of baggy brown wool trousers by Gaultier, a brown rayon top by Perry Ellis and a snakeskin belt by Hermes. As I start to dress I reflect that I must consider a final possibility: that Evan, for some reason, is pretending, equivocating, playing games with my head. Perhaps he is not made of the silly putty that I thought he was.

It's an intriguing idea.

And a rather frightening one.

I stand before the full-length mirror and tie a bright yellow scarf (also by Hermes) around my statuesque neck. All these questions ultimately don't matter, I remind myself. All I have to do is carry through the original plan.

Sitting down to put on my shoes, I try turning my thoughts to more pleasant subjects. I already spoke to the

probate lawyer and the insurance agent. I can collect the
big bucks in about six weeks, two months tops. Meanwhile
the house is on the block and so is the loft. I'm taking out
ads in the Times, the Voice, and the *Fire Island Tide*. That
reminds me, I'd better tell the real estate agents not to show
the house just yet. Not until I complete this unfinished
business. Of course they usually don't show beach houses
this late in the fall. Things will start picking up in the
spring. I guess I can wait till then to go to Vergenargue. Or
maybe I can tie up some of these business transactions from
abroad.

I'm itching to spend money. I want a total new wardrobe.
I wonder how much the upkeep is on my grandfather's
villa. Evan always took care of such details. It's such a wonderful place, I recall musingly. I love Provence—it's so rustic and decadent at the same time. I suppose I should make
some conservative investments. I'll consult Evan's broker. I
wonder why he didn't show up at the funeral. My mind
races along these lines as I brush my hair.

Should I let André tag along to France? Would he even
pull up stakes and come? I'm almost certain he would. I
have him wrapped around my pinky. It seems I always have
some high-testosterone type in that position. Maybe it's
time I tried free-lancing for a while. Well—I don't have to
make the decision just yet.

I apply make-up and slip into my Ann Klein white trench
coat. I'm in the mood for French food tonight; I'll phone
André and tell him to meet me at the *Bouches-du-Rhone.*
I'll have the *confit d'oie,* followed by a grilled *darne de
saumon.* A quiet dinner, then early to bed. Tomorrow I'll
tie up some loose ends, attend to business, make up some
alibi for the old bat. I suppose I'll have to have dinner with
her tomorrow night. What a dutiful daughter I am.

As I'm about to go out I remember that I don't have my
handbag with me. I go back to the bedroom to get it and I

think again about Jason and Evan, Chang and Eng, Jacob and Esau, Tweedle-Dee and Tweedle-Dum. I rummage through the bag to make sure that I have my house keys with me. A vagrant thought enters my mind: I remember reading once that the Nazi sadist Josef Mengele's experiments on gypsies included sewing twins together. The keys, I discover, are in the handbag and so is another object that gleams in my manicured hand.

I think, if Jason survived I may have to be extra careful. With his background he wouldn't be as much of a pushover as Evan. But I'm determined to let nothing stand in the way of my plans to snuggle into the lap of luxury where I've always belonged. I fondle the pearl-handled Smith & Wesson revolver and, before I leave, slip it into the pocket of my down parka hanging in the closet.

When I reach West Broadway I scan the horizon for a cab. Some sooty-faced pickaninny comes up to me and asks for a handout. She's about twelve years old. I counsel her to go fuck herself. A taxi glides up to the curb and I gracefully get in.

CHAPTER 23

*T*he motorboat plows the soughing surface of the Great South Bay, speeding toward Fire Island.

The pilot has given up trying to make small talk with me, the only passenger. I gave him the cold shoulder. He steers through the breaker-frayed waters as I gaze intently at the approaching dock, nestled between Ocean Ridge and Davis Park. My eyes sweep over the shuttered clapboard houses perched over the bay and take in the pines glinting silver in the twilight. The sunset makes me gasp. What a pretty picture all this makes, what a stunning backdrop for murder.

I left the jeep at home. After all why should I call unnecessary attention to my presence here? As we skim the surface of the water, spray hits my face and I mentally review the plan. It's simple, really. All I have to do is wait for the opportune moment to do it. He has no reason to suspect anything so he will not be on his guard. Disposing of the body poses the only potential problem, but I think I've worked that out pretty well.

The muscles I've developed from pumping iron should

come in handy for this operation. I'll put him in a heavy-duty lawn bag, load him into the wheelbarrow and, under cover of night, bury him in the nearby salt marsh fringing the bay. Very few people, if any, venture there, even in high season. I won't be seen; the community is deserted, especially at night. Even if the body is found—sometime down the pike—the authorities would have no reason to connect it to me. My husband has been officially mourned and cremated. Why, it was even in the New York *Times*.

I disembark on the gray wood dock, pay the water taxi driver and walk down the wood-deck path toward the ocean. I survey the scene and what I see makes me curse my luck a little. The place, much to my annoyance, is not totally unpopulated, as I hoped, and my arrival does not go unobserved. The old geezer fisherman who lives in the shack by the beach is angling off the dock. So what? My visiting the house, by itself, wouldn't prove anything. And Evan is already dead.

Leafless trees rise like filigree sculptures against the darkening sky. I climb a rise in the land where I can see the house, more visible now after the shedding of foliage and vegetation. Smoke curls from the chimney. He's there.

My eyes sweep over the ocean. It shimmers like a live thing, which indeed it is. A trawler specks the horizon. The surf foams and swirls in dark eddies around the piles of the jetty, a deep sickly green, mottled with seaweed. I shiver in my down parka and continue on toward the house.

As I walk I see the stooped scarecrow figure of the old fisherman crabbing home across the beach. The sand dunes seem to diminish and change shape in the heavy winds. I remember the weather forecast I heard on the water taxi radio: local meteorological stations had issued gale warnings for the south shore. Good. It will keep the busybodies indoors. So what if that weathered old codger was stalking around? He's nothing but a harmless beach bum, not some kind of ominous albatross.

Am I losing my nerve? I pat the revolver in my pocket. I don't think I am. But I'm human, after all. And, obviously, it's a tough thing to do. It's especially hard because I've always been fond of Evan. If it is Evan waiting for me in that house at the end of the walkway. I also grew fond of Jason, in a way. A funny thought occurs to me: this is the most ambitious undertaking of my life. In an existence devoted mainly to frivolity and self-gratification (I don't kid myself that it has been anything more), this killing will probably be my most striking accomplishment. And, if all goes as planned, nobody but I will know about it. Why does the thought displease me, even sadden me? I never thought I was the type to hanker for recognition. I guess it's something ingrained in human nature, to prefer even infamy to oblivion. To leave behind more than footsteps in the sand. I always thought I was exempt from such feelings. The sea crashing on the shore heaves up foam and the spectacle of it all, made even more impressive by the gathering darkness, matches the intensity of my troubled thoughts.

Why, for pete's sake, am I suddenly thinking about my father? I hardly ever give him a thought. Why does a picture of that handsome old sodomist suddenly enter my head? I'm told he's living in Venice now, practically a pauper, but probably having the time of his life. I envision how he must look now. His sandy curls must by now have turned gray, his ramrod figure paunchy. But I'll bet there's still a sparkle in his olive-green eyes. Maybe I'll look him up when all this is over and treat him to dinner at the Gritti Palace. Where did this streak of sentimentality come from? Am I getting soft, heaven forbid? I think it's probably more curiosity than sentiment that conjures such thoughts. I wonder if I inherited my amoral nature from him.

I am twenty yards from the house when the first flash of

lightning appears in the sky over the ocean. It begins to rain.

I try the door. It's locked so I take the keys out of my bag and let myself in, the wind keening at my back. I shut the door with a shove of my butt and lean breathlessly against it. The moaning of the wind subsides. I'm already a little drenched.

I look around me. He's not in sight. I halloo. No reply. I suppose he's sleeping. It's just as well, it gives me a chance to get settled and compose my thoughts. Am I breathing too hard? I must get control of myself by regulating the rhythm of my breathing as I do when exercising.

A pool of water running off my coat forms at my sneakered feet. With my forearm I brush wet curls away from my brow. I remove my coat and hang it in the hall closet.

I suddenly remember that I left the gun in the pocket of the parka. Fine. It's a good place to keep it until I'm ready to use it.

I walk inside, sink into the sofa and start to remove my sneakers. The fire crackles pleasantly. I take off my socks and flex my toes, basking in the warmth of the fire. From the look of the red-hot logs I would say it's been burning for at least three hours. I hope he had a cozy time in his final hours, whoever he is.

Who's who?

Which is which?

Which twin has the Toni?

I must not let myself care.

Rain patters rhythmically against the picture window, accompanied by a drum roll of thunder. I chuckle to myself: nature has a flair for the theatrical.

My stomach grumbles, craving food. On bare feet I pad over to the kitchen and take an apple from the fruit basket. I bite. It's mushy, past its prime. I glance at the rest of the fruit: the bananas are speckled, the grapes shriveled to the size of testicles after their owner has taken a bracing swim in the Bering Sea. It's apparent that he's not done any grocery shopping lately. That's good.

I toss the apple in the trash basket and go back to making a few more mental genuflections before the fire god. What am I waiting for? I'd better find out for certain where he is. Dimly I hear music coming from the bedroom. I pad over.

Sleeping like a *bébé*.

I study the face in profile above the coverlet. In repose it seems serene and innocent. It's funny how sleep pacifies human features, turning fiends into angels. I'll bet even Attila looked benevolent in his sleep. The sleeper beneath my gaze is clean-shaven and the face has no trace of fever sores or any blemish whatsoever. The music coming from the tape deck is one of Evan's favorites, a jazz piece by John Coltrane. Yet . . .

The eyes, of course, are closed now. Jason's, I recall, had a brutal kind of honesty that Evan's lacked.

What's the difference? I turn and tiptoe out of the room.

I should do it now, immediately, the booms and cracks of thunder will cover the sound, in the unlikely event that anybody is around to hear it. One well-aimed shot to the temple at close range should do the trick. His being asleep is really a God-sent happenstance. Or maybe I should say Devil-sent. It will be clean and quick, with no chance of his defending himself or anything going wrong. I couldn't have asked for better circumstances.

It would be the most merciful way too, booking him passage on a gentle cruise from sleep to oblivion. I'd be saving him from a more painful or traumatic death down the road. So, in a way, I would be performing a humanitarian act, wouldn't I? I titter to myself. How's that for a neat piece of self-justification?

Still, the reasoning is impeccable, I think as I make my

way to the hall closet. I may be heartless, but I'm not stupid. I meditate a moment on my cold-bloodedness. It's not that I'm really unfeeling, I conclude. It's just that I have a positive genius for selfishness. It's like an art form with me. Some people paint great pictures; others compose stirring symphonies; and others discover galaxies light years away.

I live a life of self-love.

I fish out the pistol and cradle it in my palm. I check the chamber to make sure it's loaded, knowing full well that it is. Then I hold my breath and remove the safety catch. No time like the present.

I carry the gun casually at my side as I head toward the bedroom. I'm not very nervous, even though I've never done anything remotely like this before. Not many people have. I bolster my resolve with thoughts of the money and the freedom on the blue horizon. In a minute it will be over. Tomorrow I will return to New York, a widow for real. Although a black widow. Next year it will be a memory. In a decade it will be a dream. What is reality anyhow? An illusion, according to many great minds. That's it, wax philosophical. But get the job done!

I think that, for the first time in my life, my palms are sweating. Didn't I say I was human?

I stop in my tracks. What's that sound? Maybe it was the high-velocity wind breaking off some tree limbs outside. Of course—that's what it was. But my certainty dissolves as the banging resumes, coming to me clearly over the sounds of thunder, wind, and rain.

Somebody's pounding on the front door.

CHAPTER 24

I am paralyzed with indecision.

The pistol seems to sear my hand. I toy with the idea of simply ignoring the visitor until whoever it is gives up and goes away. But that wouldn't be smart. The smoke coming from the chimney gives our presence away and not answering would only fuel suspicion. They might even think we're in trouble and try to force their way in. No, I'd better just see who it is.

I look frantically around for a place to put the gun. I stash it under a seat pillow of the couch. It doesn't bulge and I can easily retrieve it later. I compose myself and go over to the door.

The banging continues. There's no peephole but I catch a glimpse of him through the side transom. A man in uniform—a ranger from the Watch Hill Visitors Center. Oh great, a fed! He couldn't have picked a more inopportune time. I clear my throat and shout, "Just a minute."

The pounding stops.

I unlock the door and open it a crack. I peer at the visitor, huddled in a rain slicker, grimacing at the elements.

He tips his hat. "Evening, Ma'am."

I hesitate. Wouldn't he think it odd if I don't invite him in out of the storm and wouldn't my lack of courtesy etch the encounter on his mind? Still, I can't take the chance that he would see the surviving twin.

"Yes?" I say in a consciously brusque manner.

"Sorry to bother you, but a big storm's coming."

I glance around. "I kind of figured that," I say, unable to bridle my sarcasm.

He shuffles his feet. He's a middle-aged man with a beefy face and sad brown eyes. "Well, I mean to say, you ought to batten down the hatches."

"Is it a hurricane?" I ask.

"Not quite. But pretty close." Rain lashes his homely face. "A late tropical storm with winds high enough to knock things around pretty good, sure enough." He's shouting a little to be heard over the groaning wind. "I notice you got some deck furniture laying around."

How very observant of you, you big snoop, I think, but of course I don't say it. "Thank you, I'll take care of it."

He eyes me in a way that says he doesn't think I'm capable. "And you ought to roll down the storm shutters," he adds, waggling his finger. "That plate glass might give."

"Thank you, I'll do it right away." I start to close the door.

He puts his hand out in a gesture to stop me. "I'll be happy to help you put the furniture in the storm cellar," he says. Is that a smirk on his face? He adds, "I mean, if there ain't no man around."

He *is* a meddler! Or maybe he's just trying to be nice. Then again, perhaps he's trying to get fresh.

"No thanks," I say quickly. "I don't want to put you to any trouble."

Now I'm certain it's a smirk. He's also ogling my breasts.

He has his fucking nerve. "No trouble at all," he says, rubbing his chin.

"Thanks just the same," I say firmly and shut the door in his face. What's with these bozos anyhow? Even the ones with faces like bowls of mashed potatoes think they're Don Juan's descendants. I wait in the foyer, breathing heavily, until I'm sure that Casanova has finally taken a powder. Maybe he'll get struck by lightning.

It takes a long time before I become relatively calm again. And it doesn't last long.

"Nicole?" he says. "Is that you?"

He's standing in the bedroom doorway, rubbing the sleep from his baby blues.

So much for the merciful way.

He kisses me hungrily on the mouth while his hands wander like nomads. I yield, fusing my flesh with his, trying to be warm and responsive. At first it's an effort, but soon the hormones take hold and my indomitable erotic streak surfaces. I taste him and wonder, Evan or Jason? Surely I should be able to tell after all the years of marriage, after kisses and caresses untold. But, damn it, I'm not sure.

I push him away and scrutinize his face. Do the eyes, windows of the soul, betray his identity? No, this time they provide no clue. They lack both Jason's direct and feral gleem and Evan's crafty luster. Maybe the act of fratricide has extinguished whatever light used to burn there. "Everything okay?" I ask.

He nods. "Sure." He runs a hand through his sandy mane. "Fell asleep. I guess I had a little too much to drink this afternoon."

Sounds like Jason.

He shivers and glances toward the fireplace. "Fire's getting low. I'll throw on a log or two." He peers at me. "You hungry or anything?"

Sounds like Evan.

"Sure," I say.

"Me too. Why don't you fix us something?" He turns around and goes over to the crib to get wood and kindling. I watch him with a puzzled frown and then I sigh and head for the kitchen. As I fix a couple of turkey sandwiches (surely he doesn't expect me to miraculously turn into Julia Child), I think about how—until I'm certain of his identity—I shouldn't attempt to call him by name. If I call him "Evan" and he turns out to be Jason, then the jig is up. If I call Evan "Jason" I face a mirror image of the same problem. So I have to play it cool and neutral. Surely he'll give me a clue.

When I return to the living room I find him lighting the kindling. At a thunderclap he straightens up.

"That's some storm brewing," he says.

I place the plates on the cocktail table in front of the couch.

"It's almost a hurricane," I inform him.

"No kidding."

I then remember. "We'd better put the lawn furniture in the storm cellar." I suddenly think of a way to get the gun out from under the couch. "Would you mind doing that, honey buns, while I roll down the storm shutters?"

He lights the kindling and stokes the fire. "It can wait till I've had something to eat," he says.

"Please. It won't take you long."

"I said it can wait," he snaps.

Jason?

Of course, I reflect, Evan had a short fuse on occasion. And he's been through quite an ordeal. "Okay, it can wait," I say calmly. "Want something to drink?"

"How about some club soda?" he says.

Evan?

"I'll get it for you." I go back to the kitchen area with a swaying walk. I reach the bar, a marble-topped antique oak cabinet, and fetch a bottle of club soda. I screw off the cap and the soda hisses.

As I pour he asks, "How's New York?" I garnish the drink with a twist of lime.

"A lunatic asylum, as usual," I reply.

I hand him the glass.

"I'm glad you're here," he says, taking inventory of my body parts.

My expression softens. "Me too."

He reaches for me but I ward him off. "Not now. Let's eat first," I suggest.

He sits on the couch right where the pistol is hidden and begins to devour the sandwich. I sit opposite him on the carpet and nibble at mine. The wind whines against the windows.

I pat my lips with a napkin and say, "I'd better get up and adjust the shutters before we have natural air-conditioning."

He nods abstractedly and takes another bite.

When I return he's finished eating and is staring into the fire. He's dressed in a cotton sweater, chinos and sweat socks. His clothes are wrinkled from having been slept in.

"Another sandwich?" I ask.

He shakes his head. He gives me a quizzical look. "You've hardly touched yours," he observes.

I sit down again on the carpet and eat. "Why don't you put away the lawn furniture now?" I suggest mildly.

He shrugs and gets up. "Okay."

My heart begins to beat a little faster as I watch him walk over to the hall closet and put on a rain slicker. He has one arm in the sleeve when it occurs to me: what if somebody sees him outside? What if that ranger is still snooping around? Not likely, but possible. Why should I take the chance? I quickly try to think of a way to stop him from going outside, without it seeming odd or awkward that I changed my mind.

"Wait," I say.

He freezes, looking puzzled and expectant.

I smile seductively. "On second thought," I purr, "I'm sure it can wait till later."

A knowing smile crosses his face. "Whatcha got in mind?"

"As if you didn't know, gravy boat."

As I climb to my feet I become aware that my change of mind has been prompted by more than tactical concerns. Something in my darkly libidinous nature makes me actively want to give him a big send-off. And I've also hit on a way to settle the question of his identity once and for all. Why didn't I think of it before?

"Take that slicker off," I command him.

He drops it on the floor and advances into the room.

Let's make this something really special, I think to myself. Let's make it a fiendish work of art. I hug myself and lift my arms, removing the sweater. I let my snaky tongue flicker over my lips as I cup my breasts through the cotton fabric of the bra. With one hand I unbutton the fly of my jeans. Slowly. Then, tugging here and there, I wriggle out of them as gracefully as possible.

He stands ten paces away, arms folded, silently watching me. His expression is nearly blank, just a little misty with desire. He's enjoying the show.

That's exactly what I want.

I am down to bra and step-ins. I give him a porno-queen pout, all the trimmings. I jut out my right hip and stretch languidly. I make it part burlesque routine and part the bodybuilder's free-style posing. Although my muscles are well toned I still have very feminine lines. And I know how to make the most of them.

I turn around, rotating my pelvis, and reach back to unhook the bra. I smile at him over my right shoulder and I feel my teeth glistening with a web of saliva. I shrug the bras straps from my angular shoulders and cover my breasts with my forearms.

I turn around, making sure every motion is performed in slow, pantomimic fashion. My eyes are now glazed. The bra drops to the floor. I fondle my own breasts, covering the perky stems of the nipples with my fingertips. I widen my stance and thrust my pelvis forward. I never quite realized I had this in me.

Motionless, he drinks it all in.

Inaudibly I hum an old tune: "Enjoy yourself, it's later than you think."

I remove my hands from the nipples and shake my torso, making my breasts bounce. Then I flex my biceps in a parody of a Ms. Universe contest. With a dancer's flexibility I lift my right leg and touch the ankle to my temple, stretching the groin muscles. His eyes are still glued to the performance, and his obvious pleasure inspires me to greater heights. Or depths.

I hook my thumbs under the elastic on the waist of the panties. With an impish smirk I turn around again, presenting him with the finely scalloped form of my round rear. I bend slightly at the waist and slowly pull down the panties. I give a wiggle and step out of them. Then with a pirouette I face my prey in all my physical glory and crook my index finger at him, beckoning him to ecstasy and doom.

CHAPTER 25

I know how bad I am. I don't flinch from my own evil nature. I'm a female Judas, a kissing traitor.

My tongue reaches his rib cage and lingers there while my hand fumbles with his belt buckle. The chinos fall to the floor and he steps out of them. He's wearing no shorts and he's already as stiff as a flagpole. I descend toward his belly, determined to solve the mystery. But he doesn't let me.

Reaching under my armpits he pulls my face up to his and crushes his mouth against mine, full of pent-up hunger. His hands explore the hills and valleys of my waist, hips, flanks and bottom. Outside thunder booms over the ocean and I whimper. I don't show my disappointment. I'll surely get another chance to see whether or not he has the tattoo.

Soon the limbs of our writhing bodies, tinted rose by the fireglow, are braided on the couch. We make love, accompanied by the tin serenade of wind, rain and thunder, the raucous elements matching our excitement and lashing us to a high pitch.

We climax quickly. Afterwards he is quite still and I believe that he's dozing. The poor deprived animal! I puzzle over things. It's odd but I can't tell anything from his lovemaking techniques. But, since they're twins, it's not surprising that they perform similarly, if not identically. Now's my chance.

Our bodies are still fused. Gently I push away from him and sit at the edge of the couch. I peer at his midsection, but one of his arms is flung over the strategic spot. If I do it very carefully I might be able to move his arm out of the way without waking him. I reach out my hand.

Suddenly there is an ear-splitting crack of thunder and the lights go out.

He springs up to a sitting position. "What the blue blazes was that?" he cries.

I get up and look around the firelit room. "Lightning," I say. "It hit pretty close. Must have caused a power failure."

"Shit," he mutters. "That's all we need." He gets up and quickly puts on his pants and sweater. "Have we got any candles around here?" he asks.

"Better than that. There are two kerosene lamps in the basement. I bought them last summer."

"Where are they?"

"On the shelf in the utility room, I think. The one over the washer and dryer."

"Okay," he says, turning to go to the basement.

This might be just the ticket, I reflect. While he's gone I can get the pistol.

"While you're down there," I add, "check the fuse box, will you cute cups?"

He nods. "Will do."

I get up and stretch and my swelling hips are accented by the firelight. "My cigarette lighter's on the mantel," I tell him. "You'd better take it with you."

He grunts and goes over to the fireplace. His hand sweeps

the top of the marble mantelpiece and locates the lighter. "Back in a flash," he says.

"I'll count the seconds," I drawl.

He turns to go.

"Watch your step on the stairs," I warn.

He opens the door to the staircase, fumbles for the wooden railing and flicks on the lighter. He disappears into the darkness.

I wait a few seconds, holding my breath. There's plenty of time, I say to myself. First I get a terry cloth robe from the bedroom closet and put it on. Then, as quickly as possible in the darkness, I walk over to the couch and take the pistol out from under the pillow. The steel reflects the fire. With a sketchy smile of satisfaction I shove the pistol into the pocket of the robe and sit down to wait for him.

I don't feel nervous, just a little expectant. I hear a noise downstairs: he must have tripped over something. I put my hand in the pocket and grip the butt of the gun. I think, too bad I wasn't able to kill him while he was asleep. I really don't want to cause him unnecessary pain. But it just didn't work out that way. Blame it on that nosy ranger.

I'll shoot him in the head at close range, I reason. It'll be quicker and less cruel that way. A bullet in the brain and sweet nothingness descends. Or the soul sprouts wings and flies away, who knows? I've always been too wrapped up in things of the flesh to give much thought to spiritual matters. And the pretty leopard's not about to change her spots this late in the game. Deep thinkers don't enjoy life.

I hear another clatter downstairs. What's taking him so long?

I hold my right hand out in front of my face. It's steady. I settle back and wait, trying to curb my impatience. The pistol feels cold and hard against my curvy hip. A question occurs to me: what should I do with the weapon afterwards? Naturally I should dispose of it. I know: I'll throw it in the middle of the bay on the ride back. Pity. It's such an elegant-looking artifact.

He finally returns. "Here, hold this," he tells me, handing me a flashlight to shine in his direction while he lights the kerosene lamps.

I'm a little annoyed at his imperious tone. "What took you so long?" I ask.

He places one lamp on the kitchen counter and another on the coffee table near where I was sitting. "Took me a while to find them."

"Weren't they where I said they'd be?"

"Yeah, but they were hidden behind a bunch of things."

"What was all that noise?"

"Tripped over the fucking racing bikes."

Light flares from the lamps and I turn off the swivel-mounted flashlight and put it down near my feet. "Did you check the fuse box?" I ask.

"Yeah. The flip switches are okay. A line must be down somewhere in the neighborhood."

"I figured as much."

Combined with the firelight, the lamps illuminate the room fairly well. He sits down at the other end of the couch. I study his chiseled features, shadowed by the flickering fire. It will be a shame to obliterate such classic male beauty. Is my determination eroding? No. But it's natural for me to have mixed emotions. And, damn it, I'd still like to know who's who. It's not rational, of course. But I'd still like to know.

Before I do it.

Why? I'm not quite sure.

We don't speak. He seems preoccupied. Does he sense something? He gets up and crosses over to the rocker opposite me and sits in it. The rocker creaks, adding to the night sounds and storm sounds.

"Who are you?" I ask.

His smile looks impish in the glow of the fire. "You mean you really don't know?"

"No. I really don't."

"Then what does it matter?"

He rocks back and forth as the wind groans outside.

I inspect the fingernails of my right hand. For some reason I want to continue the game of cat-and-mouse. "I'll find out eventually," I say with an icy smile.

"Call me Blaine," he suggests.

"Blaine?"

"Yes. For Blaine Evanson, a mixture of Evan Beck and Jason Plaine, Jason Beck and Evan Plaine. What's the difference? We were one life before birth, we're one life after death."

"That's unadulterated mumbo jumbo," I say.

"Call me Blaine," he says, more insistently, with a flash of emotion in his eyes.

"Okay, Blaine. Blaine. Have it your way." He's gone off the deep end of the kiddie pool, I think with wry amusement. But I'll humor him as a last request. I'm the soft-hearted type. "I like the sound of the name."

"There was no moon that night."

"What night?"

"The night I killed him."

"Don't dwell on the subject."

"He put up a fight. A helluva fight." He touches his head where the wound was.

"Spare me the gory details, dimple buns."

"There was no moon, and the pool was dark, and the water was lukewarm."

I study his face in the dim light, but it's expressionless. It's like deciphering hieroglyphics. I don't exactly like the train of thought he's following. I slip my hand into the pocket of the robe.

He glances at the window. "Storm seems to be dying out a little," he observes.

"Yes."

"What now?" he asks.

I give him a quizzical look.

"Where do we go from here?"

Back to the womb, I think to myself, patting the pistol. I look around, unhurried. "Doesn't everything look romantic in this light?" I ask.

"I guess. But it's a pain in the ass, having no power. The food will spoil. Do you suppose it will last long?"

I cross my legs, still toasted beige by the sun and sun lamps. "I haven't the foggiest idea," I say.

"You haven't answered my question."

I pretend not to understand. "About what?"

"About the future."

For some reason I'm not ready yet to let the cat out of the bag. I spring to my feet and rub my hands together. "We've never properly celebrated our success," I say. "Let's have some champagne."

I dance on bare feet to the refrigerator where two bottles of Piper Heidseck are stored. I can feel his eyes on my expanding rear as I bend over to take them out of the dark refrigerator. His lust is palpable. I hope he's not thinking of having another go-round because he's already had his swan song. I say, "We might as well drink them before they cool off. There's some paté in here too."

I take the tray over to him and unload everything on the coffee table next to one of the kerosene lamps.

"Life's a big party to you, isn't it, Nicole?"

I grimace as I untwist the wire and deftly pop the cork, making a hiss of air escape from the bottle, the genie of the grape. "Of course, dear man. Just one long supreme bash." The champagne sizzles in the glasses. I hand one to him.

We touch glasses.

"Can I make a toast?" he asks.

I raise an eyebrow and wait.

"To our future together," he says.

I throw back my head and laugh.

"Is something funny?"

"Yes, quite funny."

His face grows grayish and he frowns, baffled.

I hold a smile. "You forget: I'm a merry widow now."

"I haven't forgotten," he says evenly.

I am displeased with myself. There's no need to be operatic about all this, I reflect. I'm being a bit sadistic. "Let's drink to freedom instead," I suggest.

"What's that supposed to mean?"

"My freedom," I say, saluting him with the glass. "You see, we have no future together. And you have no future at all."

I feel the metallic smile freeze on my face as I put my hand in the pocket and draw out the pistol. His face betrays no surprise or fear. It doesn't even register calculation, just a subtle texture of sadness.

Outside the rain has eased to a patter and the wind murmurs, accenting the shushing of the surf. The storm has sailed out to sea.

My hand is steady and my heartbeat is regular. It surprises even myself that I'm as cool as a seasoned executioner.

His face blanches somewhat. "Now I understand," he says.

"Isn't it pretty," I say, nodding at the revolver. "You know how I love pretty things." I put the champagne glass down on the table.

He sits down on the rocker again and calmly says, "You planned it this way from the very beginning."

I sigh deeply, mocking regret. "Yes. Two twins with one stone." Supporting my forearm with my free hand, I point the muzzle at his temple. I remember that long ago my father used to shoot skeet.

He rocks silently.

I feel the need to say something comforting. "Think of it this way—you'll be free too."

"How?"

"Death is a form of freedom, isn't it? Your spirit will soar."

He grunts in a dark parody of amusement. He asks, "Do you really think you're capable of squeezing that trigger? Do you have the guts to kill me?"

"I don't have to kill you, sweet stuff. You're dead already. You're a nonentity. Neat, isn't it? Nobody will even know you're gone."

"Why, Nicole?"

I keep the revolver trained on his temple. He sips champagne, nice as you please. "Why what?"

"Why are you doing this?"

"For the money, of course. The insurance money and all the rest of it."

"There's enough for both of us, isn't there?"

"And because Evan Beck was beginning to bore me. At first it was very pleasant and satisfying being married to a handsome young actor with a bright future. And I did care for him in my own little idiosyncratic way. But things started to go sour, you know? His prospects dimmed, his charms began to fade. And, on top of it all, I didn't like being tied down any more."

"You were tied down?" he says incredulously.

"Oh, I admit we had a pretty liberal arrangement. But I still felt a little bit like a prisoner."

He clucks his tongue sarcastically.

My expression darkens and I steady my hand. "Enough talk," I say.

Do I see a flicker of fear in his eyes?

"We just made love," he says. "What are you, some kind of praying mantis?"

I shrug. "Maybe." I check the safety catch.

"May the condemned man have a smoke?"

I waver. He's playing for time, of course, and I shouldn't let him get away with it. Nevertheless I relent. "Reefer or nicotine?" I ask.

"Reefer."

I go over to the mantelpiece and take a joint from the cigarette box. Still pointing the pistol at him, I hand him the jay and warily step back.

"Light?" he asks.

"Where's my lighter?"

"I must have left it in the basement. I put it down when I found the flashlight." Gripping the arms of the rocker, he starts to get up. "I'll go get it."

"Funny boy. You stay right where you are. There's a box of matches in the kitchen."

I gesture with the gun, indicating that I want him to rise. "Get up slowly. No false moves. We'll go together, with you leading the way."

As we parade toward the kitchen area he looks around him at the lamplit room, as if he's trying to hit on a plan. I must be soft in the head, going along with this. But there's no danger, really. Not while I have Messrs. Smith & Wesson trained on his brain.

We get to our destination and I motion again with the firearm. "Sit on the bar stool, nice and easy like. I'll get the matches." I stand on tiptoes and fetch a box of wooden matches from a cabinet above the sink. "Put your hands on the counter," I command. I sit down on the stool across from him, strike the match with my free hand and light the jay that is clamped between his sensuous lips.

He shuts his eyes and inhales deeply. "What do you plan to do?" he asks. "Afterwards, I mean."

I squint at him. "Why should I tell you?"

He hunches his shoulders and exhales, watching the smoke curl to the rafters. "A last request."

I shake my head. "You've had your last request. The reefer."

"Come on," he says mockingly. "Don't be so stingy with your last requests. Every condemned man is entitled to potatoes with his sirloin steak."

I poke my tongue into my cheek and narrow my eyes again. "I'm going to France. I leave in two weeks on a cruise ship."

"Sounds like fun. Are you going alone?"

I shrug and say, "I've answered enough questions, don't you think?"

"No."

I sniff the air, pungent with marijuana smoke. "Oooh. I'm getting a contact buzz."

In a mocking voice he asks, "Will it affect your aim?"

I level the revolver. "I sincerely doubt it, sugar."

He tokes deeply, then asks, "Are you absolutely sure you've thought of everything, closed all the loopholes?"

I appraise him with a touch of disdain. "I had all the angles figured from the very first day: even if the original plan goes wrong, I'm clean. You see, if Evan botches the killing I just disavow all knowledge of it. I play Miss Sweet Innocence. I'm tailor-made for the role. Then there's the possibility of Jason killing Evan. I have the bum arrested. Who's going to believe the story of a drifter with a shady background?" I shake my head. "No, any way you look at it, I couldn't lose."

"Nice."

"Very." I peer at the stub of the joint between his fingers. "You finished yet?"

"You're not in a hurry, are you?"

"Yes."

He pouts. "Just a few more tokes, please?"

I sigh. "I should have my head examined."

After a pause he asks, "Don't you still want to know who I am?"

"I'll find out soon enough."

"But you'd like to know before you squeeze the trigger, wouldn't you?"

I hunch my slim and pretty shoulders, faking indifference. "Why should I care?"

"But you do," he says, his voice rising. "I know you do."

Fucking know-it-all, I think. My finger tightens on the trigger. How does he know about my desire to identify my mate/victim before consuming him? Why do I want to know? I guess it would make the deed a more ravishing and consummate ritual act. It is, after all, my work of art.

I focus on his face in the chiaroscuro light. I think it is Evan. I say, "I think I should know my own husband." But my voice is tinctured with obvious doubt.

He shakes his head and wears an expression of superiority.

I twist my mouth in mock friendliness. "I'm killing Blaine," I announce.

He gets off the stool, turns his back on me and begins to walk over to the living room.

I level the revolver. "Where do you think you're going? Stay right where you are."

Slowly he turns to face me, a look of calm innocence stamped on his features. "I'm only going to get my champagne." He waits.

I nod and follow him. I'll soon put an end to this game.

He sits down in the rocker again, sipping champagne and smoking the reefer, a regular party boy. But I think I now discern the first glint of fear in his eyes. His actions have been mostly bravado.

I stand over him, fingering the trigger, steadying my
nerves. "You'd better say your prayers now, dearest."

He looks up at me, struggling to suppress panic, I suppose. "We could easily settle the question," he says, "If
you're curious enough."

"Forget it," I say but my voice lacks conviction.

He ignores my expression of indifference, doesn't seem to
credit it. There's too much obvious hesitation and doubt in
my demeanor. He seems to have my number in this in-
stance.

"We could settle it," he continues, "by examining the
tattoo."

I am frozen.

"You remember the tattoo, don't you?" he asks. "The
number 2 that Jason had engraved on his abdomen?"

"Yes, I remember."

He nods his head, drains the glass of champagne and
stubs out the reefer in an ash tray. Then he gets up and
starts to raise the hem of his sweater.

I wave the pistol. "Get away from there!" I warn. "Keep
your fucking hands in plain sight."

He looks wounded and bats his eyes. His hands still grip
the hem of the sweater. "I only wanted to show you by
exposing my stomach," he says. "Hey, don't worry. I'm not
going to try anything. You'll be doing me a favor by killing
me. Really you will. You'll also be killing this buzzing in
my brain that I've had since I killed him. You'll be doing
me a big favor."

It's fairly quiet. Rain is dripping off the sides of the house
and the wind is crooning. It's quiet, though, compared to
the earlier raging of the storm and the sea. I blink once or
twice, undecided. So, I reflect, the act of fratricide has mur-
dered his sleep, so to speak. It wouldn't surprise me. He's
right about my curiosity being piqued. It's more than curiosity, it's closer to an obsession. It won't be enough to ex-

amine the body afterwards. I want to know now. And he wants me to know.

I let the muzzle drop slightly. "Okay," I say. "But do it slowly. Very slowly."

He smiles and raises the sweater over his head. Then he reaches down with his right hand to tug it off his arms. The garment is balled up in his hands.

I still can't see the spot; it's lower on his stomach, covered by the waistline of his pants.

"Now undo your belt," I command him.

He nods again. Then, suddenly, he throws the sweater at the kerosene lamp, toppling it. In the same instant he lunges for me. I feel the steely grip of his right hand manacling the wrist of the hand that holds the pistol.

It flames twice in the darkness.

Pain sears my kneecap. He groans and hits the floor. I stumble on top of him, wrestling for control of the gun. The hours of training with weights now pay dividends, helping me to match him in strength. As we writhe on the floor in a burlesque of our sexual tangling I see with horror that the oil from the shattered lamp is streaming over the rug toward the fireplace. I watch helplessly as the oil ignites, sending a chain of whooshing flames darting across the room. As the room becomes a tinderbox of wood and fabric that the fire devours avariciously, the house begins to glow in a parody of a festive scene.

The pistol barks again.

The struggle ceases. He lies still.

I wait a moment, regaining my breath. Then, amid the looming shadows and the beautiful orange light cast by the raging flames, I try to regain my feet. But it's no good. I fall again to the floor, my knee a useless stew of shattered bone and severed muscle. I must crawl out. I crab along the floor, but everywhere I go the rampant fire encircles me. Oh God, oh God, is this the way it ends? I twist my face into a gargoyle. I wanted to see my father again in Venice. But now I'll have to wait, I think, coughing as the smoke invades my lungs. I'll have to wait.

Till he joins me in Hell.

Afterword

*T*he chattering blades of the helicopter stirred up heavy gusts of air that made the old man totter on his cane as he held the lure-spangled hat on his grizzled head. Gnawing on the stem of a pipe and making guttural sounds of disapproval deep in his throat, he surveyed, with eyes of pure jade, the wispy smoldering shell of the beach house.

He shook his head in dour reflection: first the drowning, then the fire. There was an elemental quality to the tragedies of this household and these people, he was thinking, though he wouldn't have expressed it in quite those words. An air of retribution by the twin gods of fire and water. So spoke his sibylline Shinnecock blood. He wondered if this was what happened to vain and self-loving people, if this was a kind of comeuppance. Is it the fate that awaits all the spawn of nymphs and river gods who ignore the ancient warning that it is unlucky, even fatal, to look upon one's own reflection in the pool? In the shriveled head of the old fisherman there seemed to echo the advice of the sages of both Montauk and Mesopotamia, spirits to whom his advanced years brought him closer and closer. He spat a blend of tobacco and saliva on the sandy ground.

Now he turned his rutted copper face toward the two stretcher-carrying medical workers who sprinted in the direction of a formless thing on the ground that only some indefinable aura marked as human. Gingerly the medics loaded the charred molt of a man on the stretcher and began to strap him in. A ranger lingered nearby. A National Guard helicopter hovered in the sky.

What a racket these helicopters make, the old-timer thought as he sucked on the pipe. He watched the corpsmen finish buckling up the patient—a very delicate procedure because of the seriousness of the burns—and he heard the ranger holler to them over the clatter of the chopper, "There's another body in the wreckage." The ranger pointed his finger. "Right over there by the fireplace. But I guess you can leave it for the coroner."

Burnt to a crisp, concluded the old man, hobbling closer to the action. The corpsmen then said something to the ranger that the half-breed fisherman wasn't able to hear. In a short time they had loaded the stretcher onto the chopper and it took off, moving slightly backwards into the air like a house fly lifts off. He mused, thinking it would be fun to fly in one of those contraptions. The rescue workers and volunteer firemen paused in their activities to watch it go.

The old man approached the ranger who stood with his hands on his hips, watching the ascent of the steel bird through dark glasses.

"Is he still alive?" the old man asked.

The ranger, who was about fifty years old, with a red face, white sidewall haircut, trim figure and military bearing, snorted, "Just barely."

"Burnt pretty bad, I guess," the fisherman said speculatively.

"Third degree all over," the ranger replied, taking off his

glasses and wiping them with a white handkerchief. He gazed out to sea where the rim of the horizon was tinted pink with the slow seeping of dawn into the sky. Then he turned back to the old man and said evenly, "You know the smell of charred steaks on a barbecue?"

The old man flinched. He got the picture. "Did I hear you right, there's another victim?"

"Yup."

"Man or woman?"

"You can't tell from the body, but it was a woman."

"How d'you know?"

"Because I talked to her last night. Came around to warn her about the storm."

"I see," said the old man, nodding at the northern sky where the helicopter was now a speck over the bay. In another few minutes, he thought, it would reach Good Samaritan Hospital in West Islip, but he doubted that the hospital people could do any good. Anyhow, he asked the ranger, "Did they say whether that joker has a chance?"

"About the same chance as an iceberg in hell."

The fisherman clucked his tongue.

"Said he might pull through with skin grafts," the ranger added.

"Oh?"

"But, nine times out of ten, they don't take."

"That right?" He dug his cane deeper into the moist sand.

"Except, they said, when the donor is your identical twin. Then you got a good chance of pulling through."

"No kidding?"

"Sure enough." The ranger turned up the collar of his uniform jacket. "Well, old-timer, guess I'll get me a cup of coffee. See you around."

"Sure, take it easy."

For a while he watched the ranger stroll across the beach,

a tall shambling figure whose outline was accented by the gold morning light. Then he turned back to gaze at the pyre that was once a house. About all that was left standing was the brick fireplace and chimney. Through the exposed rafters he could see the swimming pool, undamaged, a symbol of luxury amid ruin. Fire and water, he thought, the dual elements, natural enemies. After a while he rekindled the tobacco in his pipe and walked off, considering what to fix for breakfast.

Back in the drafty old shack on the frothy lip of the ocean, he started a fire in the pot-bellied stove and watched the flames crackle up nicely. He put two slices of white bread in the toaster oven, filled the tea kettle with water from the tap and plunked it on the burner.

He rubbed his ancient mitts before the fire.

Soon he sat down on a kitchen chair of chrome and plastic to await the harvest of his own two hands. He was content.

At the same time, some miles away in Good Samaritan Hospital on the mainland, the burn victim was pronounced dead. Every inch of his flesh had been blackened beyond recognition.